"She knows something. Whatever Ed told his wife, I'm sure she told Freda."

Logan nodded. "Possibly."

Paige stared at the storefront not really seeing anything as she groped for answers. All she knew was that the walls around her were closing in and she didn't know why.

"I'm afraid that giving this email to the state police could get me fired."

"That email might be the reason Dr. Sullivan is dead. You owe it to him to do as he asked."

Logan had such a clear moral compass. He wasn't afraid, never had been. That was probably why he was able to pull three wounded marines to safety under heavy fire.

It was also why he didn't remember them together as an engaged couple.

DANGEROUS CONDITIONS

—

JENNA KERNAN

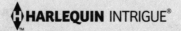

For Jim, always.

ISBN-13: 978-1-335-60478-1

Dangerous Conditions

Copyright © 2019 by Jeannette H. Monaco

Recycling programs
for this product may
not exist in your area.

This is a work of fiction. Names, characters, places and incidents are either the product of the author's imagination or are used fictitiously, and any resemblance to actual persons, living or dead, business establishments, events or locales is entirely coincidental.

This edition published by arrangement with Harlequin Books S.A.

For questions and comments about the quality of this book, please contact us at CustomerService@Harlequin.com.

® and TM are trademarks of Harlequin Enterprises Limited or its corporate affiliates. Trademarks indicated with ® are registered in the United States Patent and Trademark Office, the Canadian Intellectual Property Office and in other countries.

Printed in U.S.A.

Jenna Kernan has penned over two dozen novels and received two RITA® Award nominations. Jenna is every bit as adventurous as her heroines. Her hobbies include recreational gold prospecting, scuba diving and gem hunting. Jenna grew up in the Catskills and currently lives in the Hudson Valley in New York State with her husband. Follow Jenna on Twitter, @jennakernan, on Facebook or at jennakernan.com.

Books by Jenna Kernan

Harlequin Intrigue

Protectors at Heart

Defensive Action
Adirondack Attack
Warning Shot
Dangerous Conditions

Apache Protectors: Wolf Den

Surrogate Escape
Tribal Blood
Undercover Scout
Black Rock Guardian

Apache Protectors: Tribal Thunder

Turquoise Guardian
Eagle Warrior
Firewolf
The Warrior's Way

Apache Protectors

Shadow Wolf
Hunter Moon
Tribal Law
Native Born

Harlequin Historical

Gold Rush Groom
The Texas Ranger's Daughter
Wild West Christmas
A Family for the Rancher
Running Wolf

Harlequin Nocturne

Dream Stalker
Ghost Stalker
Soul Whisperer
Beauty's Beast
The Vampire's Wolf
The Shifter's Choice

Visit the Author Profile page at Harlequin.com.

CAST OF CHARACTERS

Logan Lynch—Village constable investigating his first murder case. He is a decorated US marine with cognitive difficulties and memory loss due to a traumatic brain injury. His position was created as an act of compassion by the town commissioners.

Paige Morris—Brilliant microbiologist at a biopharmaceutical company, Rathburn-Bramley Pharmaceuticals, and single mom, who is noticing some production anomalies at her plant.

Allen Drake—CEO of Rathburn-Bramley Pharmaceuticals.

Veronica Vitale—CFO of Rathburn-Bramley Pharmaceuticals.

Lou Reber—Head of security at Rathburn-Bramley Pharmaceuticals.

Dr. Edward Sullivan—Director of quality assurance at Rathburn-Bramley Pharmaceuticals.

Ken Booker—Director of human resources at Rathburn-Bramley Pharmaceuticals.

Connor Lynch—Logan's older brother, town commissioner and the area's only Realtor.

Rylee Hockings—Homeland Security agent investigating a terrorist network called Siming's Army.

Carol Newman—Paige's new supervisor at Rathburn-Bramley Pharmaceuticals.

Axel Trace—Sheriff of Onutake County in northern New York State.

Chapter One

Constable Logan Lynch drew on the cowboy hat that had been given to him by his older brother Connor, a village supervisor, because he said it covered the scar on Logan's forehead. Off-putting, Connor had said. "No need to frighten the kids and tourists." Plus, the Stetson made him look more like a real lawman. The board had approved his position last September. He was a village constable with no law enforcement experience whatsoever. He seemed to be the only one bothered by that. Still, he needed a job. Not much work in his hometown of 429 for a veteran with a TBI—Traumatic Brain Injury.

Most folks here catered to weekend tourists or worked for Rathburn-Bramley Pharmaceuticals.

"Morning, Constable," Paige called from across the main street.

She was so pretty and so darn smart. A real scientist, just like she always wanted to be. Meanwhile, he couldn't distinguish between a rooster crow and a truck backfiring. He wondered if she knew that her hair turned red in the early-morning sunlight.

"Don't you look spiffy. Where's your star?"

"Under my coat," he said. "It's on a chain. Nobody asks to see it anymore but you." Why had he added that?

Paige's smile blinded him. He was a deer in the head-lights.

"Big weekend coming up," she said, still walking as he crossed the street. He couldn't help it. These few minutes with Paige were the highlight of his entire day. He remembered that she had been his brother's date at his senior prom during their sophomore year. He'd been told by his dad that he and Paige had dated, too. His dad said they'd been serious enough to be briefly engaged. But he didn't remember any of that. He wished he might. If he could retrieve just one memory, it would be of them together. He and Paige were the same age, twenty-eight, and had graduated from the village's central school together. He didn't remember that either or what ended their engagement. All he knew for certain was that if she didn't want him then, she sure wouldn't want him now. She'd gone on to be a biochemist with a doctorate, paid for by her company and he was a constable who had only just regained his driver's license. All that didn't stop Logan from admiring her. She was Dr. Morris now, and a mom.

As her neighbor, he knew that she was great with her daughter, Lori. His brother and Paige were now just friends, though not from Connor's lack of trying. Logan might have to settle for that because asking her out and being turned down would kill him. As it was, he feared her concern was spawned by pity. Somehow he'd become the community project.

"You all ready?" she asked, coming to a stop and allowing him to catch up with her. She was running late today so their conversation would be brief.

"Almost. We got those..." And the words left him. He pointed vaguely at the pile of orange cones and no-parking signs that he'd be stringing up on Main Street.

The event shut down traffic for the entire day on Saturday.

Harvest Festival was a village-wide extravaganza that had everything from soapmaking to a turkey-call competition.

"Signage?" She offered the words to him as she often did. She was quick as a whip. Had three degrees in microbiology that she'd earned while he was getting blown up in Iraq.

"Yeah." He felt deflated. He might be able to pick her up with one hand, but that skill wasn't useful in conversation. His drill sergeant said his size just made him a bigger target.

Saturday, he'd be waving his big foam finger like the village idiot while parking cars in the empty lot behind the gas station and she'd be working in her research lab probably finding the cure for cancer.

"I hung that sign for Rathburn-Bramley—the company's sponsoring a lot of the festival." He pointed at his accomplishment.

Her brow wrinkled as she shielded her eyes to gaze into the early-morning sunlight at the vinyl sign strung above the street between two lampposts with nylon cording. He had learned to speak and read again but he'd never lost the ability to read emotion. Paige's expression told him that she was worried.

"Was that wise? Being in a bucket truck? I mean, your injuries."

"Damage done, my doctor says."

"Still, another head injury…" Her words trailed off.

"Not good for anybody, I suppose." He grinned and then stopped, fearing the dopey smile that always seemed to come to his face when he was around her made him look damaged. He adjusted his hat farther down his forehead.

They had been in the same class most of primary school. He remembered that with the clarity of a cloudless summer sky. But he couldn't remember much past junior year. He'd lost the time between his junior year and when he woke up Stateside at Walter Reed about six years later, along with the part of his brain that allowed him to hear and talk and read. Reading came back first. Speaking more slowly. The hearing was improved, though the doctors said he still didn't process sound correctly, might never process it as he had. He'd adjust, they'd said; he'd learn to speak more slowly to give him time to recall the words, but the memories were just gone.

He was glad the hat covered the worst of the scar. It kept Paige from staring at his forehead. Now she stared at his hat instead.

"You…ah…you be there on Saturday?" he asked.

Paige always made him more tongue-tied than usual.

"Planning on it," she said.

"They're bringing in a bouncy hut this year," he said.

She turned from the street and faced him. "You looking forward to that?"

"No. Not me. The kids. I hope." He sounded more like a guy without a brain than one with a brain injury. "Your girl might like it."

Paige looked away. "Lori is too old for that, I'm afraid."

Why would a woman with an eight-year-old daughter care about a bouncy hut? Lori was already on the youth soccer team and he noticed she was fixing her hair now instead of leaving it in a wild braid with strands flying everywhere. Unlike Paige's hair, Lori's was light brown and her eyes were amber. Like her father's, he supposed.

That thought brought a frown. He'd asked Paige once about the girl's father and it had made her cry. He wasn't doing that again.

He stared at those sympathetic blue eyes. Paige had skin that was rosy and perfect. She was taller than most women with a frame as willowy as a dancer's. She'd been five feet eleven inches in eighth grade and gotten no taller. She'd even been taller than he'd been for a time. Until sophomore year when he'd shot up to six feet and one inch. Back then her red-blond hair had been to her waist. Now she wore it at chin length, letting the riot of curls just dance all around her pretty face.

He tried to ignore the smell of her skin and the urge to feel the soft texture of her spiraling curls. She stared at him with those bewitching blue eyes. He went still as his body galloped to life. He wanted to break their friendship by kissing her, really kissing her, and take this relationship back to what he'd been told it had once been. But he was equally terrified that doing so would ruin what they had. He lived on their friendship, tried to make it be enough. What if he told her how he felt and she laughed or avoided him?

Paige was a scientist. Educated. Pretty and a mother. While he was a brain-damaged vet who had gotten his head knocked in "engaging insurgents while simultaneously evacuating three wounded marines under fire." That sounded cool and he surely wished he could remember doing that. But it wasn't as cool as the fantasy of being Paige's one and only again.

Why would she settle for a man like him? She wouldn't. He knew it and that stopped him every time.

"Well, good luck setting up that bouncy hut," she said.

He tipped his hat and she smiled, letting her go yet again.

And she was off, walking down Main Street from the home that she shared with her parents from the time they went to school together. Only now her dad was gone. So was his mom. Paige was a scientist at Rathburn-Bramley and yesterday he'd mistaken the church bells for the fire engine.

But he and Paige had always been close; he had looked out for her and now she looked out for him. She'd even helped his brother get the village council to approve his position, with some assistance from her new employer. She'd helped him get the necessary certificates and training to be a constable, too. He missed her helping him study. He wondered again if he should try to kiss her. Then he imagined making an unwelcome advance and decided it would be a great way to end their friendship permanently. She didn't want a man like him. Who would?

"Have a great day, Dr. Morris," he called.

She paused, half turned, glancing back over her shoulder at him. "And you have a great day, as well, Constable Lynch."

Paige Morris hurried down the street, wishing she could go back in time and change things, knowing she could not. Each misstep along the way, each decision that seemed like the only option at the time, rose up to haunt her now.

For the best, her mother said. But was it really?

The stone in her heart ached as she reached the entrance to the manufacturing facility, waving at Lou Reber, who was the head of security. She registered her identification badge on the scanner as Lou watched the monitor for the green light.

Lou had the lined face and gravelly voice of a former

smoker, a muscular build and the gray hairs to prove he'd worked as a police detective for twenty-some years before he earned his gold shield and took his early retirement from the force in Poughkeepsie, New York. Somewhere along the way his grown kids had stopped bringing the grandkids to visit each summer, but he had been married to the same woman for thirty-four years, so he was doing something right.

"How is Miriam?" His wife had suffered a fall on a ski slope a few years ago and had injured her back. Two surgeries later, she still couldn't do any of the activities she once enjoyed like gardening, golf and skiing. As if that were not enough, she had been recently diagnosed with kidney failure and required biweekly dialysis down in Glens Falls.

Lou's smile slipped. "Oh, about the same. Good days and bad days. She's on the list for a new kidney now." He exhaled, his expression glum but then he rallied. "You hear about the hunters up on the cutoff from Turax Hollow Road?"

"They shoot each other?" she guessed.

The location had a fair number of hunters from urban areas who did not quite seem to know the difference between Jersey cows and deer. They also sometimes shot at motion that could be a deer or their hunting partner.

"No, they ran into a bull moose."

"With their car?" Paige knew that at 1,300 pounds, a bull moose stood six feet high on stilt-like legs and was the perfect height to sail over the hood of a car or truck before crashing through the windshield and crushing the driver. Everyone up in the Adirondacks had a healthy respect for moose.

"No," said Lou. "They were *chasing* it down the road. Animal got tired and turned to fight. Guess they figured out how fast that truck could go backward!" He laughed. "The thing put his antlers through their windshield."

"They're big animals."

"And meaner than all get-out in mating season, which it is." Lou pulled out his phone. "State police asked me to tell everyone to be extra vigilant while driving. They also sent me photos. Want to see?"

She nodded, and Lou went to his texts. Up came an image of a blue pickup truck missing its passenger-side mirror, with deep gouges in the side panel. The windshield was caved in like an empty soda can and the glass showed a web of hairline cracks.

"Wow."

Lou beamed, delighted at the damage. "Village supervisor voted to close that cutoff to traffic so folks avoid that moose's territory."

She approved of that solution. Calling animal control would mean that moose would be put down. The hunters had been in his territory. The long-time village supervisor and Logan's older brother, Connor Lynch, was competent and respected, handling squabbles and avoiding small-town politics with the mastery of an experienced politician.

Paige wished Lou a good day and headed for the elevator. Once inside the compartment, she unbuttoned her wool coat. Today was one of those in-between days. Too hot for winter gear and too cool for a light jacket.

Leaving the elevator, she crossed the spotless hallway and tapped her card to the contactless entry system that allowed her access to her department. Two more such barriers and she was in the peace and quiet of her lab and hanging her coat beside her coworker's. Jeremy Chen generally beat her in since he did not have a daughter to see off to school. Getting Lori out of bed was becoming a challenge that she suspected would get worse as middle school loomed.

"Where's Ed?" she asked Jeremy, referring to Dr. Edward Sullivan. Her boss, and the head of product quality assurance, was generally here at six in the morning because he said that was the only time he could get anything done. Then he left at three so he could coach his son's travel basketball team over in Mill Creek.

Jeremy glanced up from his computer. He was her height, ten pounds lighter and of Chinese descent. He wore his straight black hair short on the sides and long on the top. He had a habit of pushing his bangs back off his forehead when thinking, only to have them fall back in place the instant he removed his hand. Only his protective glasses ever managed to keep his hair back from his face.

Jeremy glanced at the clock on his computer screen. "Wow, he's really late. I'm not sure where he is."

"You got that report done?" she asked. The monthly quality control statistic compilation was Jeremy's job.

"I need Ed's results from the last round," he said.

"Want me to get it?" They all knew each other's login information as the company had yet to adopt a file-sharing system that worked. The bugs in the current one caused it to take forever to transfer data and, as flash drives were not allowed by company policy, they had resorted to this workaround.

"No. It can wait."

Her department did all the quality assurance testing for all pharmaceuticals produced on site including liquids, gases and solid tablets.

Paige stowed her lunch in the mini fridge and her purse beneath her desk. It wasn't like Ed to just not show up.

"Maybe I'll call Lou." She already had the handset to

her ear. Lou confirmed that Ed had logged in at 5:37 a.m. and left at 6:00 a.m. to do his run. But he had not checked back in before Lou arrived at eight, and Lou had not seen him since arriving. She lowered the phone. "That's odd."

Paige relayed Lou's information.

"Call Ursula?" Jeremy suggested, referring to Ed's wife.

"Maybe." Paige retrieved her mobile phone and considered her options. She didn't want to worry Ursula unnecessarily. "I'll try his cell." She did and got his voice mail. "It's Paige. Call me back when you have a chance."

Something didn't sit right. It was dark out when Ed ran and there was no shoulder on most of the county roads. He could be lying in a ditch right now. Then she thought of what Lou had told her just this morning and sucked in a breath.

"Does he run on the cutoff on Turax Hollow Road?"

Chapter Two

Lou Reber showed up at the lab just before lunch wearing a long face and rubbing the back of his neck. There was no clearer indicator that he was the bearer of bad news.

"What's happened?" asked Jeremy, meeting Lou half-way across the room.

Paige instantly thought something had happened to his wife, Miriam. The woman was so changed since that ski accident, distracted, disheveled and unfocused.

But then she realized as the pit of her stomach dropped like a broken elevator, the bad news was about Ed, her boss.

"We found Dr. Sullivan," he said. "Constable Lynch drove his jogging route after we couldn't find him. He's... gone...dead. Looks like a hit-and-run."

Paige sank to her seat on the high black stool beside the tall lab table, samples abandoned as she absorbed the blow.

"He's got kids," said Paige, her voice trembling as the shock of having this man so suddenly torn from her life met with denial. As if having kids somehow exempted him from premature death. Hadn't her father's fatal auto accident taught her that no one was immune from tragedy?

Jeremy picked up where she had dropped off. "His

son's team… He coaches for the Lions Club and Boy
Scouts." Jeremy's head sank and he covered his face with
both hands.

"Everyone… The whole village will be devastated,"
said Paige as the denial gave way to grief.

"That's certain," said Lou. "Anyway. That's all I know.
Lynch is out there. He's with the game warden who was
in the area because of the moose. They're waiting for the
state police and the county coroner."

"Does his wife know yet?" asked Jeremy.

"Logan's been to the Sullivans' home and told Ursula. She is headed to the school to pick up her son and
daughter."

"Logan's sure it's Ed?" asked Jeremy. His voice was
soft, as if he couldn't believe what was happening. Neither could Paige.

"Listen, that boy might not be all there but he sure
knows every family who lives in Hornbeck and a fair
number that don't."

"He was always good with names," said Paige and
both men stared at her. She realized then that she'd spoken of Logan in the past tense as if he were the one who
had died. Sometimes she felt like he had. Part of him,
anyway, the part that loved her.

"Did he die right away?" asked Jeremy.

Lou shook his head. "Doesn't look that way."

Paige gasped. Could Edward have been saved if the
driver had stopped or if help had reached him? If they had
reached him, she thought, taking personal responsibility.

"I should have noticed that he was late," said Jeremy,
shouldering the guilt.

"I didn't notice he had not checked back in," said Lou.

Jeremy's head hung and his gaze fixed on the floor.
"But I did."

"It's not your fault, either of you," said Paige. But she wondered if one of them could have saved him. If she, or either man, had noticed soon enough, called, checked and found Dr. Sullivan before the minutes of his life ticked away and he died, abandoned, on a lonely road.

IT WAS HARD not to notice when the village's new EMS vehicle, carrying her boss's body, made its way past the manufacturing plant. Paige's lab was on the second floor and though the plant was three blocks off the main street and down the hill, she saw the flashing lights of the procession of the state police cruisers and EMS truck. The bright red and blue lights blinked in the twilight. Paige realized, grimly, that the ghastly parade would pass directly before Ed Sullivan's home. Would his wife and two children be there to watch?

Her phone blipped, relaying a text. She had been getting texts and phone messages all day. She glanced at her mobile's lock screen and saw that it was three in the afternoon and that she had received an incoming text.

She stared at the message as icy fingers danced up and down her spine. Dr. Sullivan wouldn't have taken his phone on his run, but he'd have his smart watch. With no cell service, the text could not be sent until the watch returned to the area where internet service was available. Here, at the company, their Wi-Fi cast a net all the way past the volunteer fire department. So if the watch was still with his body, the message from him was being sent now. She shivered.

Paige watched the EMS truck, imagining Ed's bloody corpse and the watch, still sending her his message.

She unlocked her phone and checked the message, which was a series of emojis. Easier to send than typing out words, even with phone prompts. Had he been injured, dying, when he wrote this or was this before his accident? She hoped, prayed, it was before as she stared at the three emojis and one typed word.

The message was composed in the following order: a green box with a white check-mark emoji, the word MY written in capital letters, the computer emoji and finally, the face with a zipper for a mouth.

That message was crystal clear. Ed wanted her to check his office computer and keep quiet about it.

For what?

The possibility that Edward's death was no accident flashed in her mind as her skin stippled in fear. Each tiny hair on her arms lifted like a warning flag. They would check his watch. They would see the message. They would know she received it.

Paige dropped her phone as if she suddenly discovered a ticking time bomb in her palm, because she had. Ed had just died. He'd sent a message about something on his computer. Part of that message was to keep whatever she found quiet. She began to feel that text was as dangerous as any toxin they kept in the lab.

Ed had shown her that the watch did not lock until removed from his wrist, his corpse. If it were stolen, the watch would remain locked. But Ursula might know his passcode. The police would check his messages, at the very least. Would his killers?

She tried to calm herself. She was making a big leap here—from a possible hit-and-run to outright murder. And over what? Something on his computer?

Just what had Dr. Sullivan gotten himself into and why was he dragging her along? She glanced wildly about. Her gaze fixed on the flash outside her window. There, like a bright beacon against the gathering gloom of storm clouds, the EMS vehicle's lights blinked as the van reached Main Street and turned toward the funeral home. That was where they'd take Ed before any autopsy. Inside the flashing truck, her supervisor's body lay strapped to a gurney. She closed her eyes at the image.

Call the county sheriff or check Edward's computer?

She reached for the phone to call security. Lou Reber had twenty-three years' experience as a detective in Poughkeepsie, New York. He'd know what to do about this.

Paige had the receiver at her ear with the dial tone buzzing when she realized that was exactly the move that Ed Sullivan would have made if he found something illegal. He'd call security.

But now he was dead.

Lou had a staff of four. Any one or all of them might be involved. Involved in what? Was she crazy to blow this up to DEFCON 1?

Breathe. She tried but her lungs felt like someone was squeezing them.

You're smart. Think.

It was hard to concentrate past the buzzing in her ears.

She lowered the phone to its cradle with a trembling hand. Balling her hand into a fist hid the tremor but not the aftershocks that rolled through her body.

The computer check came first. Her throat closed against the scream that turned to a squeak at the realization that she was going to check his computer.

"Paige?" Jeremy's voice held concern. "Are you all right? You've gone pale."

She'd worked with Jeremy for four years. He was her best friend here at work. But did she know him…really know him?

Her father used to say that you would be lucky to have maybe one friend you could call to help you move the body. Jeremy was not that friend. And what would she be dragging him into if she told him?

No one knew anyone that well. If her suspicions were correct, telling anyone might involve risk. Grave risk. But so would telling no one. That watch. The one with the messages was out there, linked to her.

"Just upset. You know. Trying to get my head around it all."

"I know. I feel sick."

Did he? He looked just fine.

What should she do? If she used Ed's computer, Jeremy would notice, especially if she was on there for an extended period.

There was no *if*, she realized. Only when. She would check his computer and she would leave an electronic trail by doing so. There was no avoiding it. Her gut told her that Jeremy was not involved. With time speeding by, she made her move.

"I have to check something." She walked as casually as she could to Sullivan's computer on legs that seemed to have turned to chalk.

Once she had decided to do as Edward had asked, there was no turning back. She sat at his computer and opened File Explorer, scanning the list of recent files. She was aware of Jeremy's gaze.

"Are you sure that's a good idea?" he asked.

"I don't know. But I'm doing it anyway," she said.

His eyes rounded, but he said nothing more as he busied himself with the tasks before them, preparing the samples for quality testing.

Meanwhile, she wondered what Dr. Sullivan had been involved in and worried that, whatever it was, she was now also involved. That, alone, was reason enough to explain her trembling, bloodless fingers.

Dr. Sullivan had been a caring boss and a friend. He was…had been a good scientist. If he was the victim of a tragic accident, then none of this mattered. But if something nefarious was afoot, she had tied herself to the railroad tracks. She knew nothing about cloak-and-dagger affairs. She knew science.

And her hypothesis was that Dr. Sullivan had been murdered. Proving that theory might just get her killed.

She continued to scan the alphabetical list of files, fixing on one. A chill danced like a dropped ice cube down her spine, but she opened the file titled Testing Anomalies and scanned the contents.

Chapter Three

The state police had given Logan the terrible job of noti-fying Ursula Sullivan of her husband's death. The man in charge, Detective Albritton, could not have been clearer that he did not want or need Logan's help.

Logan had stayed with Mrs. Sullivan until her younger sister arrived and then headed to the office, leaving the two women to collect Ursula's kids and tell them the terrible news. Logan covered the phones while the state police took care of securing the scene and began their in-vestigation of the hit-and-run. They told him not to give out any information except that there had been a traffic fatality. But most folks calling already knew who and where and how.

No one knew who had hit Dr. Sullivan and left him in the muddy jeep track to bleed out.

And no one asked why. Except him. Why did such a good man have to leave his family?

There was a chiming sound like a child repeatedly hit-ting the metal panels of one of those rainbow-hued xylo-phones. His brain played tricks on him. Sound was the worst. The doctors explained that his hearing was per-fect but the place where the sound was supposed to be sorted into useful categories was damaged. So he often couldn't distinguish between a siren and a ringing phone.

He could tell the direction, and that helped. After that he just had to make his best guess. The office phone was easy as it had a flashing red light. His cell phone was more challenging. All the rings and dings and chirps sounded the same, so he didn't know if he was answering a call, text or message.

He kept waiting to be what he was or what he thought he had been. His doctors said that wasn't going to happen. There was no going back. Forward was the only option and finding what his doctors called "a new normal."

But being the village mascot was demoralizing. He lifted his phone, saw nothing on the lock screen and then tried the office phone, which was flashing again.

"Hello. Constable's office. This is Constable Lynch speaking."

"Logan, what happened out there on Turax Hollow Road?"

Voices were another challenge. He could no longer distinguish male from female or familiar from stranger. It annoyed people, especially his father.

"There was an accident—" The caller cut him off.

"I know that part. Is Dr. Sullivan dead?"

"The names of those involved won't be released until after the families are notified."

"I'm *your* family, Logan. This is your brother, Connor, who is also village councilman. So tell me what happened."

"Oh, sorry, Connor." His problem caused some people to think he was no longer very bright, his brother included. He just wished he could get back to old normal.

"Okay. You're sorry. Now, what happened?"

Connor was a village official, so he gave him the info. "Dr. Edward Sullivan was struck by a vehicle and died at the scene. Hit-and-run. That's all I know."

"Idiots," muttered Connor, then to Logan, "Who is handling the investigation?"

Not me, thought Logan. "The state police, and I just saw the county sheriff's vehicle drive past the window. So they're all out there." The light of the emergency vehicles drew his gaze from the desktop and the doodles on his blotter that looked like one of Paige's pale blue eyes, framed with long, dark lashes. He stared through the storefront window of the former video rental place that had been turned hastily into the constable's office here on Main Street after his position was approved. "EMS vehicle is coming up Raquette Road now." He could see them reaching the junction of Main. "Seems like all the law enforcement vehicles, too, state police, and I think that's the mayor's Subaru. Guess they're done at the scene."

"Fabulous. Where are they going?"

"Owen's," he said, mentioning both the largest residence and only funeral home in the village.

There was a sound like a ringing or perhaps a song.

"Connor?" His brother did not answer.

Dial tone, he decided and returned the handset to the cradle. Then he stepped out of the office to watch the procession making the turn. The last vehicle was a white SUV driven by the sheriff of Onutake County, Axel Trace, who had not even bothered to check in with the village constable.

Logan stepped out to the street and removed his hat as they passed and came upon Paige's daughter, Lori Morris, walking from school with her grandmother. With all the excitement, he'd lost track of time. He glanced at his watch and saw it was already a little after three in the afternoon.

He turned to Lori, dressed in a purple polar fleece jacket that added bulk to her thin frame. "How was school?"

Lori looked away from the retreating procession of official vehicles.

"Mr. Garrett got called away so we had Mrs. Unger," she said and made a face.

Logan joined her, twisting his face as if he were poisoned. Mr. Garrett was Lori's teacher, and a volunteer with the fire department. He was also a paramedic. And Mrs. Unger had been his primary school principal, as well. She had been universally disliked back then based mainly on her position of authority but also on her tendency to be nicer to her charges whenever a parent was around. Since leaving school, Logan had gotten to know Mrs. Unger, who also volunteered with the fire department, and had grown to admire her. She was silver-haired and tough as any US marine he had ever known.

"Still looking over her glasses at kids?"

"Yes!" said Lori and rolled her golden eyes and then did a fair imitation. "I don't know what she was talking about. We're studying plants and she was talking about comotosis and phototosis or something and I think that's high school stuff. And she is *so* boring! She makes *me* comotosis!"

He laughed. Lori was funny.

"Mitosis and photosynthesis?" asked her grandmother, impatience making her voice tight.

"Maybe," said Lori.

"And this—" she waved a finger at Lori before continuing "—is the sort of nonsense that caused me to have to speak to her after class." Mrs. Morris turned to Logan.

"I don't see why I should be punished for my granddaughter's disrespect."

His brother's new "dragon-orange metallic" Audi Q8 model SUV raced by, exceeding the speed limit. The color looked to Logan exactly like the orange flashing light on a snowplow. He frowned.

Mrs. Morris watched the SUV disappear after the procession. "You should give him a ticket." Then she directed her cool gray eyes on Logan. "Shame about Dr. Sullivan."

Word traveled fast.

"Did Paige call you, Mrs. Morris?"

"You can call me Beverly, Logan, as I've told you."

He looked away, uncomfortable with that. He'd always think of her as Paige's mom, Mrs. Morris, despite her insistence that he call her by her first name.

Mrs. Morris sighed. "Yes, she did call."

"What happened to Dr. Sullivan?" asked Lori.

The two adults exchanged a look. Logan shook his head. He wasn't speaking about this before an eight-year-old. The world had too many monsters, but the ones under her bed would do for now.

Mrs. Morris clearly felt differently for she answered the question.

"Your mother's supervisor has been in an accident."

"Is he okay?"

"No, I don't think he is."

"What kind of accident?" asked Lori.

"I'll tell you on the way home." Mrs. Morris set them in motion. Lori remembered to say goodbye and waved a hand sheathed in a mitten fashioned to look like a zebra puppet complete with a braided tail and pink lolling tongue. The googly eyes rolled, making it look as if it also had a head injury. Logan waved back. Then he replaced his hat and returned inside to the phones.

He made it only to the new wheelchair ramp and paused at the sound, unsure what it was. He could identify where it came from, toward the village library, on the corner of Raquette and Main, in the former home of the Hornbeck family. The village's namesake had founded the bank back when the railroad stopped in this village. The sound reminded him of a fish thrashing in the river after it was hooked. But it turned out to be Paige Morris, hurrying along Main, passing the autobody shop and the antiquarian bookstore.

She wiped her face every few seconds with her gloved hands. Today was cold and windy, and Paige had a blocked tear duct. He remembered with perfect clarity in the winters of their childhood that the tears rolled down her left cheek and froze on the collar of her maroon nylon snow coat. Funny how he could remember that but not a minute of his time in the US Marines or a minute of his engagement to Paige.

But Paige's tear duct dripping did not make a noise and she was making a noise. Was that pain? He crossed Main Street to intercept her. She usually walked home after five but was early today.

It wasn't until he was nearly before her that she noticed him. The noise she was now making was obvious. Paige was crying.

Chapter Four

Paige hurried up Main Street with her head down against the wind and her shoulders bent by the weight of her troubles. Someone stepped directly into her path, bringing her up short. She startled, glancing up. Instinctively, her hand went to her shoulder bag and the printed copy of the file she had found on Dr. Sullivan's computer.

Logan stood before her.

For just a moment he looked as he always had, back when her family had been in trouble and he'd done the wrong thing for the right reason. One look into Logan's sympathetic eyes and she fell to pieces.

The years of his absence disappeared. Pain and fear lowered her resistance and she stepped into his arms, sobbing. He was just the right height to cradle her against his chest and rest his chin on the top of her head. His familiar scent comforted her as tears rolled down her cheeks like raindrops down a windowpane.

"Why are you crying?" he said. "Is it Dr. Sullivan?"

She couldn't have answered if she had wanted to. And she couldn't tell him what had happened. But she wasn't sure who to tell about the text message or what she had found afterward. She wasn't even sure what the document meant, just that it highlighted an inconsistency. Inconsistencies were the enemies of quality assurance.

Dr. Sullivan had found something. She suspected he reported his concerns to the head of security or to his supervisor, Sinclair Park, or even the CFO, Veronica Vitale, and then he had died.

A correlational relationship. Not necessarily causal. But she could not eliminate, out of hand, the possibility of causality.

"Is this about Dr. Sullivan?" Logan asked again.

Paige nodded, snuggling closer to the canvas jacket supplied to Logan by the village.

Logan cradled her against him. "I'm sorry about Dr. Sullivan, Paige."

Nodding, she managed to rein in the sobs. Logan helped coach Ed's son on basketball. He'd lost a friend, as well. Her coworker's death would leave such a hole in the community. And his kids…his wife…

Her ragged breath and a hum in the back of her throat was all the sound emerging from her.

"He was a good man," said Logan.

"He was."

"They had the state police up there. County sheriff, too."

Since they were a village of only a little over four hundred residents, they could not afford a police force. But after Logan had come home, his brother, then newly appointed to the village council, raised concerns that traffic had increased with the arrival of the pharmaceutical company two years before, the company that Connor himself had helped advocate for. Rathburn-Bramley expected the village to manage the increased traffic flow and issues arising from the daily commute of the workforce of two hundred employees, nearly all of which lived outside their community. The taxes they paid more than covered the cost of the salary of the new village constable, the hiring of whom had caused debate in the village, narrowly winning out over the placement of a traffic light on Main. Rathburn-Bramley also covered the cost of a new hook-and-ladder fire truck, EMS vehicle and emergency equipment for the volunteer fire department, continuing to make yearly donations. The company seemed interested in a good public image, and they were willing to pay for it.

Now the village had both a well-equipped volunteer fire department and a constable, who was fully trained according to New York State law. Finding a doctor to pass Logan on the medical exam had been a challenge, but Connor had managed that, too. His brother had wisely ridden the wave of pride generated by Logan's heroism. As a Silver Star recipient, Lance Corporal Logan Lynch made his hometown proud. Because of his accident, no one expected him to do much but direct traffic every afternoon and march in the village parades.

"They'll find who did this," said Logan.

"I doubt it," she whispered.

"What?"

"Nothing."

He drew back and dropped a kiss on her forehead, then drew back again, his face registering worry. Perhaps he thought he had overstepped.

"I'm sorry," he said.

"Don't be." She'd enjoyed his tender touch, a reminder of his protective care of her at a time long ago.

He looked relieved. "I'm glad you walked this way."

This route was slightly longer than cutting across Railroad Avenue and then turning up Turkey Hollow Road to Main. But she walked it daily so she could see him. He'd often walk her home, then return to the office next to the hair salon or, on evenings when she was running late and he'd finished directing traffic, he'd simply walk her home and then head to the house next door to hers. Like her, Logan had never moved out of his childhood home. He and his dad, now a widower, lived in the big yellow farmhouse north of her mother's place, a white, two-story home that had been there for a hundred and fifty years. Both farms had barns large enough to hold a few cows and a plot of pastureland behind that was big enough to keep them fed summer and winter. The cows had been moved out long ago, before Paige or Logan's parents purchased their houses. Paige's dad had been a dentist until his death in an automobile accident during her junior year in college. Logan had lost his mom just after he had turned eleven.

How old were Steven and Valerie Sullivan? Paige tried to remember Ed talking about their birthdays. Steven would turn fourteen this December, old enough to try out for the JV team next year. That made Valerie…eleven. The same age Logan had been.

The ache in her heart pulsed with every beat.

Those poor kids. She was glad they had Ursula. Their mom was strong and capable. She'd be there for her children.

Paige rested her head on Logan's shoulder and her arms hung at her sides. He patted her back while she tried and failed not to long for more than comfort from him. She lifted her head to gaze up at his big brown eyes, looking again for a flicker of recognition. She went still as her body galloped to life. Everything inside her wanted him to kiss her. Except he didn't. He never did. The top of her head did not count.

"Why don't you think they'll catch who did this?" he asked.

"I'm afraid I don't have the faith in the system that you did. Do," she corrected. "Never have."

"If you hear anything, Paige, you should tell me."

"I should," said Paige. But she wouldn't.

She felt she couldn't rely on Logan anymore, ever since he'd left for Iraq years ago, not telling her he was reenlisting until it was too late.

Now all memory of her as the love of his life had been blown out of his thick skull.

After her dad died, she and her mom struggled financially, and she really didn't know if she could finish her undergraduate degree. With no life insurance and in deep debt, her father had left her mother and Paige in dire straits, with only bankruptcy protecting their home.

Even so, it was her father and mother's mess. Not hers; certainly not Logan's. She'd told him that and that she'd figure it out. But Logan had done what he thought best. Without consulting her. Reenlisted and volunteered for the higher-paying combat duty. She could have strangled him then and now.

She had told him, at the time, that she believed life decisions that affected them both should be discussed. He thought her ungrateful. He said he was taking care of things. The disagreement that ensued had turned ugly and he'd asked for his ring back.

She'd been so shocked that he would break their engagement especially after her father had just passed away, but she had done as he asked and returned the diamond solitaire. Logan had left for Iraq and she had not seen him again until after his accident.

"You can trust me, Paige."

"I do trust you." But inside, she just didn't count on him anymore. He had improved. Was it enough to try again? She gazed up at him, wondering what he'd do if she just kissed him already. Maybe that would jog something loose inside that brain. Like the reverse of the prince kissing Sleeping Beauty.

She reminded herself how grateful she was he'd come home at all. When she'd first learned of his injuries, though, she thought he was gone in a different way, never to return. His doctors told his family that Logan would probably not be capable of caring for himself. But she had disagreed. She'd gone to him at Walter Reed and stayed right up until her due date.

When he'd finally come home, Paige had been there. But after Lori's injury, people who knew they'd been together urged her to move on, not to burden him or herself with trying to recover memories of a relationship that had broken up anyway.

She'd tried. She still did. Until moments like this when she wanted him to remember everything, to be awakened by her touch, her kiss. But that wasn't how brain injury and recovery worked. Some things were just gone forever. She had to accept that.

Sleeping Beauty, she thought and smiled. Logan was still beautiful. The scar didn't change that. His dark, fathomless eyes and crisp, thick hair still tempted. Even that stupid cowboy hat made him look as handsome as any Western hero of movie or television.

She paused to face him. He pushed back the brim of his hat. She used her teeth to tug off one glove and then used her index finger to trace the hard line of his jaw. His coarse whiskers gently scraped her finger pad. She gave him her best seductive smile.

And for an instant, he was back. His eyes went wide with speculation and then came that easy, slow smile.

A familiar garish, orange Audi SUV raced by them and made an illegal U-turn right on Main. Connor Lynch pulled to a halt at the curb, and the passenger window whisked down. Logan's brother leaned across the seat to peer at them.

As if caught doing something illegal, Paige jumped back from Logan and now glowered at Connor. He used to make a habit of interrupting them whenever he thought they might be…occupied. Some things never changed.

"Paige, you need a lift home?"

She stiffened and narrowed her eyes at Connor. This was yet another attempt to keep her away from his little brother. He'd made his feelings crystal clear after Logan finally came home. Logan was not capable of that sort of relationship, Connor had told her in no uncertain terms. And she should not burden him with trying to have one. Connor had been adamant, she'd ignored him and Lori had suffered as a result.

She'd backed off, but stayed close, watching his gradual improvement. He might not remember her, but his accident had not reduced his intelligence. Even his doctors said so. The slow speech and hearing trouble were results of brain injury. The part of his brain that handled cognitive function had been unharmed. Most people around here forgot that. Spoke to him more slowly than necessary and as if they were dealing with a child or a pet monkey. It infuriated her.

But was that indignation on his behalf or fury over what she had lost? She didn't know, and sometimes her disappointment over Logan reenlisting blended into a general anger at the universe for stealing something precious from them both.

"I can walk her home," said Logan to his big brother, his speech slow by comparison.

"Aren't you supposed to be directing traffic at five?" he asked his kid brother.

"Yes. But I have time to walk her home and get back."

"Today we need you in your office to cover phones. We had a traffic fatality. You still have a job, bud. Don't blow it on me."

"I can walk her and then come back. I didn't take a lunch today."

Connor ignored him. "Paige. Get in the car."

Her home was half a mile east on Route 10, but she wasn't sure she could make it, even leaning on Logan. She was equally sure that she didn't want to ride with Connor. Ever since his little brother came back from Iraq, Connor had been trying to move in on her. Not that his little brother noticed because he'd forgotten her with the rest. Logan might not remember what they were together, but she did. And Connor was not Logan's replacement. She'd told him so, more than once. All the cars and boats and fancy houses in the world wouldn't change that.

Logan drew back as if anxious to put her aside again.

"It's getting cold. Windy," he said and glanced toward his brother's car. Logan could drive, but his truck was parked back beside the office.

She stared up at him, willing him to recall something, anything, as she had so many times before. The betrayal of his forgetting them as a couple, as an engaged couple, of him forgetting he told her that he loved her forever and would make this all right, hurt in her bones. That betrayal had mellowed into a pervasive longing and soul-deep aching sadness. It hurt to look at him sometimes, especially when she was remembering, and he was just giving her that congenial smile.

Still, she had to wonder, who did she seek out when she was in trouble? Not Connor, the village councilman with a successful business in real estate and a large empty house of his own.

She'd come to Logan.

"Paige, I have to talk to you," said Connor.

Her radar engaged. What did a village councilman have to talk to her about? She decided right then that she was not speaking to him or anyone else about what she had found until after she had reread the document from Dr. Ed's folder.

Logan opened the passenger-side door, and Paige reluctantly slipped inside. She gave his free hand a squeeze, but he didn't return it as he once would have.

Connor took his foot off the brake, and she waved to Logan, whose brow knit as he lifted a hand in farewell.

And then she was being whisked down Main Street, toward her mother's home, her home again, too.

She still couldn't believe she was back here in Hornbeck. That had never been her intention. Neither had getting pregnant her senior year of college. Her mother disapproved of Paige's decision to keep the baby and stay close to help with Logan's recovery. But Lori's accident forced Paige to face facts. What choice did she have? She'd needed to earn a living and care for her daughter, so she'd accepted the fellowship at Cornell and earned her master's degree in only one year. Next came an opportunity in Arlington, Virginia. But when her mom had been diagnosed with breast cancer, Paige had come home to find Logan much improved, a fact that no one in his family or her mother had shared with her. The job at Rathburn-Bramley allowed her to stay. That had been four years ago. They had even paid for her doctorate. And here she was, still, close to Logan and waiting for him to come back to her.

"What are you doing, Paige?" Connor asked.

She gave him a blank stare.

"You tried this. We all were against it, but you told Logan everything and he forgot it as soon as you told him. How many times?"

"Six," she lied.

"More like ten."

"He's doing better," she insisted. "No lapses in short-term memory."

"Great. So what if your daughter calls for help and Logan thinks it's the television again?"

The memory made her stomach clench. Shortly after he returned to his father's home, Paige had been visiting with Lori, then ten months old. Paige had stepped out to retrieve a package from the mailbox, leaving Lori happily perched on Logan's lap. When she returned, she heard her daughter wailing from outside and ran into the house to find Lori on the floor, a gash on her chin. Logan stood before the lounge chair pointing the remote at the television as he vainly tried to turn off the volume. He thought their baby's howls of pain were on the television.

"It was too soon," she said.

"It *always* will be," Connor replied. "You should listen to us this time."

Before they reached the old white farmhouse, they passed the funeral home where Dr. Sullivan's body likely now lay in the basement on an aluminum table. He should be finishing up at the lab and heading home for supper. She shook her head in despair. The authorities would have to do an autopsy. That thought gave her the shivers. She checked the connection on her safety belt again.

"What did you tell Logan about today?"

"Tell him? Nothing."

"That's good. Just upset him."

While she appreciated his concern for his little brother,

Connor was the one who seemed upset. His face was red and he kept dragging his fingers through the hair on the top of his head. Connor looked much like Logan with just a little thickening at his waist and hair that was lighter and noticeably thinner. His skin was ruddy, and tiny burst blood vessels in his cheeks pointed to a drinking problem. Too many meals alone at the pub and too many evenings alone in his big, empty house, he had once told her. If that was supposed to make her feel guilty, it didn't. No one told him to buy that B and B.

"How did you hear about Dr. Sullivan?" Connor asked.

"Lou told us."

"Lou Reber?"

She nodded.

"I heard from Freda. We were going over the agenda for the board meeting when Ursula called."

Freda Kubr was Ursula Sullivan's sister, a village councilor and the administrative assistant to Principal Unger.

"And Lou told you how he died?" he asked.

"Hit-and-run."

"Did you see Dr. Sullivan today?" he asked.

"Not today."

This began to feel like an interrogation, as if Connor was constable, and it made her uneasy. Why was he so interested in these details?

"I'm sure the state police will want to speak to you. They told me they'll be interviewing all his coworkers."

"Why? Wasn't it an accident?" she asked. She had her suspicions, but she wanted to see his reaction.

"That hasn't been determined yet."

How did he know that?

He swiped a hand over his mouth and then returned his hand to the wheel. She'd never seen him this jumpy.

"Did he say anything to you or was he behaving strangely?"

"Not as strangely as you're behaving." She twisted in her seat to face him. "What is this about, Connor?"

"We've never had a case of manslaughter in Hornbeck before. It is going to be in the papers. Most people who live in this county don't even know we exist, and the village likes it that way. I know Rathburn-Bramley does. It's why they picked us for the plant."

It was true, Paige knew, that even people living in the same county didn't know that this little turn in the highway was a village. Both the railroads and the major highways had left them behind years ago. This was an advantage to a company who produced controlled substances. Hiding in among the farms and hills made perfect sense.

Connor banged his hand on the steering wheel. "They'll mention where he works."

"No secret where he works. Is there?"

"Your company prefers a very low profile. Can't see it from the road, so the tourists and visitors certainly don't know it's here. Draw the wrong people, it gets out what you all are cookin' down there." He glanced at her. "You know exactly what they produce."

"I should. I test every product on every run."

"Well, then you also know that opiates are a target. They don't want to be on the map."

Her company also produced fentanyl and a variety of intravenous drugs and gases used by anesthesiologists. Most had a high black-market value and were favorites of some addicts. Ironically, they also produced innocuous medical supplies like aerosol disinfectant spray and gel hand sanitizer.

"Well, they can't just pretend he wasn't killed," said Paige, addressing Connor's concerns with sarcasm.

"Your employer is requesting he be listed as unemployed. His widow has agreed."

"That's sick." And a shock. She could understand the company's desire for a low profile, but this seemed to take it too far.

"They offered her money. A lot of it, above and beyond what she'd get with the company's life insurance."

"But they think this was an accident? Right?"

"Maybe. But his ID tags are missing."

Her eyes widened. Had he been killed for his access key?

"But they can't get to the manufacturing area with that and they can't get past security. They check our photo against the tag."

"What about after hours?"

"Tag is time sensitive. Six a.m. to six p.m. Plus, you need a special card to access the finished goods area. After hours you need an escort. One of the security team. They'll deactivate his access. I'm sure they already have done so." As soon as the words were out of her mouth, she regretted them. She shouldn't be revealing security measures, even to Logan's brother.

"Sheriff and the state police are looking for his tags and the vehicle that hit him. Anyone you know want to hurt Dr. Sullivan?"

"No! Of course not. Everybody loved him." She felt a jab in her belly as she recognized that she was already referring to her friend in the past tense.

Connor made a face.

"What?"

"I overheard Lou speaking to Dale Owens at the funeral home. Lou told him that your firm was investigating

Sullivan. Something out at the plant was going missing. They were getting ready to fire him."

"That's ridiculous." She again peered at Connor. He seemed to have done a fair amount of nosing around already. Why was he so interested in this? Was it just because he was concerned for the town's reputation?

"They were onto him."

"He'd never steal from his employer."

"Maybe it was intellectual property. Like a process or formula. Could he have known they were onto him?"

"Are you suggesting he stepped in front of a vehicle and then stole his own ID tag as a cover-up?"

"Of course not." His hand raked his hair again. "It's just, we've never had a thing like this happen here. I helped bring that plant here, Paige, and I feel responsible for it and any trouble that comes because of this sort of industry. Could have been a bad drug deal or something."

"Nonsense."

"We are a peaceful village, Paige. Cows, cornfields and…"

"Opiates," she finished.

Chapter Five

Paige got home to find her mother cooking dinner, which was unusual. Her mom had made it very clear when Paige moved back in with her that she was going to raise her own daughter and that meant housework, errands and making her child's meals. Her only concession had been picking up Lori after school because Hornbeck Central School did not have an after-hours keeper program.

"Where's Lori?" asked Paige.

Her mother continued stirring white sauce on the stovetop as she half turned to speak to Paige.

"She's out back making a leaf pile and then jumping into it. Malory is watching her from the porch."

Paige did not think that Malory, her mother's long-haired cat, was an adequate babysitter, but a glance out the side window showed her daughter tunneling through dry leaves in the spotlight of the backyard floodlight.

Paige set her satchel on a chair at the breakfast table and removed her coat and scarf. Then she folded into the adjoining chair. Her mother brought her a bottle of scotch and a small juice glass and set it before her.

She gaped and then met her mother's serious gaze.

"You heard?"

"Whole village heard. That ogre of a company let you go a few minutes early today?"

Paige lifted the glass. The strong, distinctive aroma reached her before she took a sip and grimaced. The liquid burned all the way down.

"I took some personal time."

"You should take tomorrow. Those pills can wait a day."

"I don't make pills." She set the scotch aside and wiped her watering eyes.

"I know what you do. I paid for some of that fancy education, remember?"

It was impossible to forget.

"Though I expect our constable will have the culprit arrested in no time. That is if he doesn't mistake the church bell for the fire truck again."

One of Logan's early blunders was to head over to the fire station at noon his first day when he thought he heard the siren. It had turned out to be the bells that the Methodist church rang every weekday at noon and at ten a.m. on Sundays.

Paige ignored her mother's jab at Logan. She was used to them.

"I've been over to see Ursula this afternoon," said her mother.

"How is she?"

"She looks terrible. But her sister is there, and Freda told me that they are accepting callers tonight and tomorrow."

"Tonight?"

She was surprised. They'd only just learned, and Paige thought they'd still be processing the shock.

"Freda said that Ursula does not want to be alone. The church is organizing casseroles to be delivered each day. Mine is tomorrow, chicken tetrazzini casserole. I think

I won't add the cayenne. I don't know if the Sullivans like spicy food."

Paige's hopes of dinner vanished.

"I'm making enough for us, too. I should bring some to Albert, feeding that man-child." Albert Lynch was the widower father of Connor and Logan. And the man-child, she assumed, was his brain-damaged son.

"Logan is not a man-child." Paige's voice was sharp. "He is just as smart as before."

"Hmm. Then why does he talk so s-l-o-w?" she asked, drawing out the last word.

Paige knew exactly how smart she and Logan both were, with her breakup with Logan after she discovered he'd reenlisted and then sleeping with him again her senior year in college before he'd shipped out. Nobody in Hornbeck knew he'd been to see her at school. She'd been so angry at him and scared for him and it had just happened.

Nine months later Lori had happened. She'd picked the name to honor Logan. Hoped they'd have a chance at a second start after she finished her undergraduate schooling. His plan had not included being wounded and nearly dying. And hers didn't include giving up on him. Their families had convinced her to stop telling Logan about Lori's paternity when he couldn't remember anything new past a few hours back then. She'd agreed, but she had continued to bring Lori for visits. Seeing their baby brightened Logan. Only she believed that Logan could handle the responsibility of caring for a daughter. As it turned out, she'd been wrong.

She'd ignored them and Lori now had a scar on her chin that served as a constant reminder that Paige was not always the best judge where Logan was concerned. Her emotions and hopes were too tied up in his being able to love her and their daughter to allow her to be unbiased. Now she feared trying and failing again with him. She'd given him time, years to recover. He didn't forget things anymore. His speech had improved, and he was working now. It seemed dishonest not to again tell Logan about their relationship and his daughter. She'd have to tell them both eventually, especially when it seemed Logan no longer forgot things. She'd been waiting for Lori to be old enough to understand that her father had a TBI. Was an eight-year-old capable of comprehending this?

Maybe his father would agree with her that it was time.

"If you weren't so stubborn, you'd…" Her mother's words trailed off.

Paige tried to ignore the urge to ask her mother to finish her sentence, knowing that she wouldn't like what she had to say, and failed.

"I'd what?"

"You would stop following Logan like a puppy and pay a little more attention to Logan's older brother. Connor's been sweet on you for ages and he's asked you, I don't know how many times, to go out with him. He's got a thriving business and a political position. He has that big house that I'm sure he bought because he knows you love it."

"That isn't true." But even as she said it, Paige suddenly feared it was true. "Logan is Lori's father."

Her mother sniffed. "Who can't tell a baby from a remote control," she muttered as she continued the rhythmic stirring.

Connor was the smart choice; any of the single, employed professional men at Rathburn-Bramley would be. She'd been asked. She'd said no.

Because she was an idiot. Because she didn't love Connor. She loved the man who had left her behind. That man had not come back. As for Connor, fondness and guilt were poor foundations for a relationship.

Paige thumped her elbows on the table and cradled her forehead in her hands.

"Lori deserves a father, Paige. One qualified to care for her."

She pressed her mouth closed to keep from lashing out. Her daughter did deserve a father and had one. It was Paige's decision to keep them apart. And it was a decision she reconsidered daily as Logan improved.

"He's not going to remember you, Paige. He's just not and he never will. And even if he did, do you want to be married to a man who earns his living at the benevolence of others? He's the village idiot."

Paige pressed her hands flat on the table and rose to her feet.

"Mother, if you ever call him that again, I will take Lori and that job offer in South Carolina."

"Might be better for you if you did. Better than seeing you mooning around after that boy."

Paige gaped. She'd never expected her mother to call her bluff.

"Mom, is that what you want? For us to go?"

"I want what I've always wanted—what is best for you. And that boy never was and never will be."

LOGAN FINISHED DIRECTING the rush of vehicles leaving the company lot and funneling up to Main to then head toward Mill Creek to the east or Ouleout to the west. After he stopped back in his office to lock up, he headed toward his blue 2004 Ford pickup. Then he made his way home. The temperature had dropped, and he worried that it might rain on Saturday. That would put a damper on the Harvest Festival. If this kept up, they could even have snow on their big day.

Instead of stopping at his home, he passed it and turned down Cemetery Road, crossing the West Branch of the Raquette River and then heading along River Street. Dr. Sullivan had lived in a Dutch Colonial home just outside the village. He had planned to only drive by but found cars and trucks parked in the drive and on the lawn. The porch was lit up and callers spilled across the porch and down the steps.

He parked across the road, off the shoulder, and headed over to the property. Logan tipped his hat and murmured hellos to the familiar faces and didn't even try to focus on one speaker or another. With so many folks conversing at once, he just couldn't identify who was talking. He passed Mr. Sinclair Park, who stood on the steps. He knew that Paige's department reported to him, because she'd once pointed him out as her boss's boss. He worked at the plant, something in production, and had moved to Hornbeck soon after being hired about the same time Logan started as a constable.

"Logan," said Mr. Park. "Paying your respects?"

"Yes, sir."

"That's a good man." Park slapped him on the upper arm as if he were a draft horse.

Logan stepped in from the cold and into the bright hallway. He removed his hat and gave it a spin before unzipping his constable jacket. He had intended to find Mrs. Sullivan, seeing her in deep conversation with her sister, Freda, in the living room, but then he spotted both Sullivan's fourteen-year-old son, Steven, and eleven-year-old daughter, Valerie, sitting with their chins on their knees on the steps leading to the second floor. Instead of the familiar basketball shorts and sneakers, Steven wore gray slacks and a black shirt, and Valerie was wearing a forest-green skirt and white blouse. He'd never seen them in this sort of attire.

Steven's chin lifted when he spotted Logan, assistant coach of his travel basketball team.

"Coach," he said, his expression hopeful.

Logan changed direction and headed up the stairs, pausing to sit two steps below the kids. He placed his hat on the same step.

"I'm sorry about your dad, Steven, Valerie. He was a really good coach."

Valerie didn't make a sound, but tears sprang from her eyes and rolled down her cheeks.

"You going to be our coach now?" asked Steven.

"I don't know. Probably."

"Everyone keeps hugging me," said Steven, his expression now cross. His lower lip and the break in his voice told Logan that Steven was on the verge of tears. A swipe of his sleeve across his eyes confirmed Logan's guess.

"It's okay to cry, Steven. When my mom died, I cried for months. Not all the time but a lot and sometimes when I didn't expect it. I'd just start crying."

"How'd she die?" asked Steven.

"It was an aneurysm in her aorta." He pointed to his heart. "That's like a bubble in the artery. The wall of that blood vessel is thick and tough, but my mom's was thin there and when it let go she died very fast." Right beside him at the grocery store just after he turned eleven. He remembered the way she'd fallen, as if she had been a marionette with all the strings cut at once. The grapefruit in her hand had rolled straight down the aisle in the produce section like a bowling ball. He'd hit his knees beside her and stared at her face. She'd looked so surprised. But she'd already been gone.

"Where is my dad now?" asked Valerie, shaking him from his dark memories. He wondered if the child meant metaphorically or physically. As he pondered how to answer, Steven cut in.

"Nobody will tell us," said Steven. "They just say he's in heaven. Or with God. But where is he really?"

"Do you mean his remains?"

They nodded in unison, eyes wide.

"They took your father's body to Owen's funeral home. They have beds there for folks who have passed. And since it was an accident, the state police need to have a look at him for clues to help them catch whoever did this."

"And put him in jail," said Valerie.

"Might be a him," said Logan. "Might be a her. But we're trying every way we know to catch them."

"Is he cold?" asked Valerie.

"No. Definitely not."

"I've only ever seen dead animals. They get all stiff and swollen," said Steven.

"No, that won't happen. The people at the funeral home will wash him and dress him and treat his body respectfully."

"Why?" asked Steven. "He can't feel anything now. Can he?"

"It's more for the family. Rituals to take care of our dead. It's a last act of love."

"You ever seen a dead body?" asked the boy.

Logan had seen many, according to his military record, but he remembered only one. "My mother, when she died and then again the day of her funeral."

"What about at war?" asked Valerie. "Dad said you

were in combat and that some of the other soldiers with you died."

He'd been awarded the Silver Star for valor after half the roof had caved in on him and his men in a building in Fallujah.

"I heard that, too. But I don't remember any of those deaths because I got hit in the head," he said as he pointed at the scar on his forehead as evidence.

Both the Sullivan children regarded the scar with serious concentration.

"Kids in my class say you got a metal plate in your skull and you can stick a magnet on your head and it just stays there."

"No plate, so a magnet wouldn't stick."

"Steven, Valerie?" Mrs. Sullivan stood at the bottom of the stairs, holding the newel post and looking up at them with red-rimmed eyes. Their gazes met. "Mr. Lynch, I didn't know you were here."

He retrieved his hat and placed it over his heart as he stood. "I'm really sorry for your loss, Mrs. Sullivan. I had great respect for your husband."

"Thank you, Logan."

"He'll be missed." He descended the stairs, and she extended her hand. The circles under her eyes and the red, puffy eyelids made her look years older. He kissed her offered cheek and drew back.

"Thank you for coming. Have you had your supper? We have too much food." She took hold of his hand and led him toward the dining room, but paused in the hallway to stare at him. "My husband was having some trouble at work this week. He told me that he was worried about something. Running helped him relax." She spoke quickly as if she'd been bursting to share the information with the right person.

"What?"

"Anomalies. Missing samples. That's what he said."

Someone stepped up behind them.

Lou Reber, the plant's head of security, moved from the living room into the hallway, and Mrs. Sullivan's eyes widened. She spoke to Logan without looking at him.

"Go and fix a plate for yourself, Logan, and please take something back for your father."

Reber came up to her and took her hand, expressing his condolences. Logan hesitated a moment and then stepped into the dining room where callers mingled around the overladen table in quiet conversation.

In the hallway, Reber moved toward the front door. Mrs. Sullivan glanced to Logan and then approached.

"Would you ask the sheriff to come see me tomorrow?"

"I can call him right now."

Mrs. Sullivan glanced about the house, filled up with friends and members of the community.

"Tomorrow is soon enough." She left him, returning to the living area through the arched opening connecting the two rooms.

Logan filled his plate and sat on a folding chair beside Donavan Bacon, a cook at the Lunch Box who had no shutoff switch when it came to alcohol. Bacon didn't drink regularly but when he did, usually on Wednesday after his bowling league, Logan was often called to bring him home because drinking made him want to fight. Donavan greeted Logan warmly. He was such a nice man when he was sober.

After emptying his plate, Logan headed to the kitchen to deposit his glass in the sink. From the doorway he spotted Lou Reber in the hallway, heading up the stairs. He thought he'd left.

Likely to speak to the children who were sitting on the stairs, as he had done. But when Logan returned to the hall it was to see the children were not there and Lou was descending the empty staircase from the second floor.

Logan scowled, wondering why the man had gone upstairs when there was a powder room off the hallway.

"Hey, Logan. Rough day today, huh?"

"Sure was. Why were you upstairs?"

"Bathroom," said Reber.

"There's one down here."

"Occupied." He looped a thumb over his belt. "Did you know Sullivan?"

"Coached at the school with him."

"Oh, that's right," said Reber. "I knew that. Dangerous to run on our roads. No shoulder."

"He was on the cutoff. Wide dirt road. Shouldn't be any vehicles back there."

"Hunters use it." He glanced toward the door. "I've got to go. You need a lift home?"

"Got my truck."

"That's right. You drive now. See you around, Logan."

Logan watched him go, unsure what bothered him about Reber's going upstairs.

He let himself out a few minutes later, but not before one of the ladies made him a plate for his father. In his truck, the aroma of food tempting his taste buds, Logan headed back up River Street to the steep incline on Cemetery Road. Ed would be buried there, probably next Saturday.

On Main he turned toward home, knowing that just beyond lay the funeral home and Ed Sullivan's body. The autopsy was scheduled for the morning down in Albany, New York. The county had a contract with the medical center to perform such duties, and Dr. Brock Koutier, their coroner, had ordered it be done. As a result, the funeral would not be until next Saturday, giving the county enough time to transport Sullivan to and from Albany and then back up here to Owen's for final preparation.

He slowed before the three large maple trees that stood as sentries between the road and Paige's mother's home. He pulled into the driveway between his dad's and her mom's properties, parked and then headed toward the kitchen door, but paused to breathe the cold air and glance toward his neighbor's place.

The lights of the Morrises' upstairs were all on and the porch light was off. Paige was home safe. He knew her bedroom sat on the west side of the house up front nearest the road, her daughter on the east and Mrs. Morris in the back near the stairs. There was a wide, flat roof that stretched over the ground-floor porch from the back of the house to the front, under Lori's window. On the porch below, the rocking chairs creaked and rocked in the November wind. Paige's bedroom had no roof beneath either of its two windows. He knew because there was a time when he'd thought about seeing if he could climb that big old maple tree out in front to her window and throw rocks at the glass. He'd decided against it. He wondered what would have happened if he had tried?

Movement caught his eye and he stepped off the road into the driveway. Something big moved down along the side of the house and into the shed that led to the backyard.

Was that Mrs. Morris? The figure had been too large to be Paige.

Propelled by an uncomfortable feeling, Logan walked to the shed, but found no one there or in the backyard. He knew their kitchen door was locked and the light off. The front door was also locked. He circled the entire house twice more and saw no one.

Had he seen anyone in the first place?

Chapter Six

Logan stood in the Morrises' yard, staring at the house. Then he retrieved his phone and dialed Paige. She answered on the first ring.

"You home?" he asked.

"Yes, why?"

"Everything all right?"

"Logan, what's wrong?"

"Thought I saw someone in your yard. I'm out here but there's no one now."

"Just a minute."

He heard Paige moving, rustling and a squeaking like a kitten looking for its mother. Several minutes later the light in the living room flicked on. He watched Paige, dressed in a lavender polar fleece robe, move from the living to dining room and then through the kitchen. Finally, she returned to the living room and opened the door, the phone disconnecting.

She called to him from the front porch, half in and half out of the screen door. "I just checked on Lori and on Mom. They're both in their rooms. Everything is fine down here."

"Call if you need me," he said.

"Thank you, Logan." She closed the door and he heard her throw the bolt.

He walked across the yard to his truck and retrieved the plate of food that Mrs. Sullivan had sent home with him, and carried it to his dad's place. The sweet odor of decaying leaves filled the air, but there was no rustle as the leaves had been pulverized by his dad's mower since he had left for work this morning.

The only light on in his house was the one in the hall and the bluish glow from the television as his father watched a talent show on cable.

"Hey, son. You're home late." His father didn't know. All this had happened, and his dad had likely been mulching leaves.

Logan offered the plate.

"What's this?" The way his dad blinked his eyes told Logan that he'd dozed off in his recliner.

Logan told him everything as his father held the plate before him, still covered in plastic wrap.

He sat with his father a while, but, restless, Logan drew the blanket off the back of the couch to go outside and look at the moon.

Who was he kidding? He was going to stare at Paige's window and watch to see if anything moved on the Morris property.

"Going out to listen to that hoot owl?" asked his dad, referring to the great horned owl that lived up the hillside.

Logan couldn't tell the difference between an owl and the wind chime on the Morrises' porch.

"Yeah. Getting some air," he said and headed out to sit on the porch steps.

The brown bats no longer darted across the sky. They lived up in the barn on the hill. Too cold, he decided, and the insects were all gone. They'd be hibernating now. He missed them flitting and darting overhead. The November air felt bracing as he sat on the porch, facing Paige's window, which had gone dark.

He wondered why Paige and his brother didn't make a go of it. He knew they had attended his brother's senior prom. Paige had been excited to attend. Sophomores were only permitted to the school's biggest event if they were invited by a senior. He remembered her dress and her mother taking photos of the couple right there on the steps of her home while he sat here watching. She wore a gown of mint green and her hair up with a few tendrils of curls floating about her shoulders. The color of the dress, her red hair up and festooned with fresh flowers and her translucent skin all combined so that, to Logan, she looked like the queen of the fairies.

She'd been stunning. And now she was a beauty. They'd been a couple once. Everyone said so. He wondered what she'd do if he asked her out. Laugh at him, probably.

No, she'd never. It would be worse. She'd be unfailingly kind as she said no.

He gripped the blanket more securely about his shoulders and tightened his jaw. Everyone said he was different now. But he didn't feel different. He accepted that he was less able in some ways, all of them associated with his brain's temporal lobe that controlled language, hearing and memory. The early frontal lobe problems he'd experienced with movement, short-term memory and concentration had resolved themselves. He was lucky. The doctors all said so, often. But those other issues were likely permanent. Still, everyone kept waiting for something to change and for him to go back to the man he was. The one everyone missed.

One thing that hadn't changed were his feelings for Paige. Those had just grown stronger, their friendship ripening into love—for him. The difference now was that he knew he wasn't worthy of her. And her mother hated him. She hadn't always. He'd have to ask Paige what he had done to earn her cold disdain.

He was glad for Paige's friendship, but he wanted so much more. The question was, would he risk that friendship trying to take their relationship in a more personal direction? Connor had done that more than once. Logan had watched him repeatedly try and fail. Now Paige avoided him when possible and suffered his company when she couldn't. He thought that might kill him if she treated him like that.

Logan stood and looked to Paige's window and the maple tree he had never tried to climb.

ON FRIDAY MORNING Paige was greeted at work by the head of security, Lou Reber, who was uncharacteristically somber-faced. Her first thought was that he was mourning Ed, as they all were, but then her mind went in more suspicious directions. Did the company know that she had logged on to Edward's computer and that she had opened, read and even printed several of his files? She needed to speak to the state police, but her efforts to reach the lead investigator of last night had failed and she was waiting for a call back.

Lou directed her to the second-floor conference room and said that the CEO of Rathburn-Bramley would be speaking to all workers on the day shift in a few minutes. Entering the large room, she found all seats at the table already occupied mostly by the brass. The rest of the administrative employees stood outside the inner circle. She moved beside Jeremy Chen and glanced about the table.

Ken Booker, the head of human resources, fiddled with his glasses and the pages in the folder before him.

Allen Drake, the CEO of Rathburn-Bramley, sat at the head of the oblong table exhibiting his customary confident smile and dressed in a crisp charcoal-gray suit that clashed badly with the bluish-brown of his dyed hair. The man was short and fit, but clearly in his sixties. Paige thought the unfortunate color choice did not make him look young and vigorous but rather pale and older than his years.

Beside him was the only woman in the group, the CFO, Veronica Vitale, who had given up her red power suit and bright lipstick for a more appropriate navy suit and simple, natural makeup. Vitale seemed to have lost weight since the last time she wore that suit. All the smoking, Paige decided, noting her dry skin and the flashing yellow teeth that reminded Paige of a rodent.

Sinclair Park sat to her left. The production manager oversaw all manufacturing operations. He worked a swing shift, covering the end of the night shift and the beginning of the day. His hours often bled from one to the other and he had the circles under his eyes to prove it. Beside him sat their plant's safety director, the business director and then a woman she did not know. She was an attractive brunette with shoulder-length hair carefully styled and frozen in place with some hair product. Her suit was an interesting pale gray with undertones of violet picked up by the deep purple silk blouse. Her gray eyes fixed on Paige for a moment and then flicked away.

A few more of the production team, the guys from shipping, and Connie, who oversaw the finished goods area, slipped in as the CEO rose from his seat.

"Thank you all for joining us. As you have likely heard, we have suffered a loss. Dr. Edward Sullivan, our head of the quality assurance team, was killed in an automobile accident yesterday morning. Police are investigating and we are asking you to answer their questions if you are called for an interview."

Mr. Drake continued with kind words about Dr. Sullivan and the loss to the community. He was an excellent orator and covered all the appropriate information, speaking as if he knew Ed well, which he did not. His words on Edward concluded with information on the funeral, scheduled for next Saturday at 10:00 a.m. followed by a private burial. Calling hours for the Sullivan family would be next Friday evening from six to eight and next Saturday afternoon following the service at the Methodist church.

"The family has requested no flowers but that donations be made in Edward's honor."

Paige realized that Dr. Sullivan, instead of attending the Harvest Festival and then coaching his son's basketball game on Saturday, would instead be waiting in Albany's morgue for an autopsy.

"Perhaps you will think us hasty with our newest hire, but with our new products coming online and the fourth quarter earnings in mind, the board and I have brought in a highly qualified individual to step into the role of senior quality assurance specialist."

Jeremy gave her a look, as shocked as she was that overnight, they had replaced Dr. Sullivan, especially since Paige or Jeremy could have handled the responsibilities, even applied for Ed's job at the appropriate time.

"This is Carol Newman." Drake motioned to the woman in the purple blouse. "Carol, stand up, please."

Paige didn't hear all of what came next because she was overcome with sadness for Dr. Sullivan—all he would miss and how he would be missed, and how quickly the company execs were moving on. She did catch that Carol had worked in the Ohio branch of

Rathburn-Bramley in the same department, and then they were dismissed, to Paige's relief. She needed to get out of that room and process what she was feeling and what had just happened. Ed was gone, and they already had a replacement?

Paige almost made it out when Vitale called her and Jeremy back. Both of them were introduced to Dr. Carol Newman. Paige felt she was making a fool of herself, barely able to keep the tears from streaming down her face, so Jeremy did the talking for them both until they were finally released to get to work.

Jeremy was the first one into the office, holding the door for Paige. She was still wiping her eyes, which now burned, and blowing her nose as she entered and ran straight into Jeremy's back.

"Whoa!" he said.

Paige glanced up and saw what had brought Jeremy up short. Dr. Sullivan's workstation had been stripped. Already. "They took his computer," said Jeremy, pointing.

Paige's skin began to tingle. She glanced toward the door, resisting the urge to run. Instead, she swallowed back the lump in her throat.

"They took everything. It's like he never even existed," said Jeremy, his arm falling back to his side. Then he turned to her. "Is that normal?"

"I don't know."

"I mean, looking at it would make me sad, too, but taking everything, it also seems wrong. Do you think it's because of the investigation?"

Paige shook her head, at a loss. She didn't know. She only knew that she was in deep trouble. What would happen to her daughter if she was fired? Paige began to recalculate the cost of following the directions in Dr. Sullivan's text.

She made it to her stool before her knees gave out. What was she going to do?

"Paige? What's wrong?"

"Everything." She was on the verge of telling Jeremy, but then she stopped herself. If he was involved, telling him was dangerous. If he was not involved, telling him would be dangerous to him.

She decided to try the state police once more, and she pulled out her cell to call the number now in her recent call list but not wanting to let Jeremy know what she was up to, she stepped out of the office.

She needed to reach a state police investigator today. She'd text an excuse for her absence to Jeremy later.

Unfortunately, Dr. Carol Newman caught her at the elevators and turned her right around.

"I was hoping to get brought up to speed," Dr. Newman said with artificial cheer. "Shouldn't take too long. I've heard good things about you."

The entire morning was spent on getting Carol current with their projects. The woman asked the usual questions, and showed some gaps in knowledge of all the processes they used for quality-assurance testing. She seemed especially sensitive to the difficult situation into which she had been thrust. Paige almost felt sorry for her until she saw her sitting at Dr. Sullivan's place at the lab table.

Paige glanced up at the security camera that covered most of the lab, except the sample storage area. She'd never really thought about the glowing red eye that captured everything, but that was because, until today, she'd never had anything to hide.

Chapter Seven

Logan got the call around ten in the morning from Sheriff Trace to find the coroner and bring him to Dr. Sullivan's house. Trace told him that he had tried the funeral home and gotten the machine and tried the doc and gotten his voice mail.

"What's happened?" asked Logan.

"Just get him and bring him here." The sheriff's voice held irritation and then the call disconnected.

Trace hadn't asked for Dr. Koutier, the general practitioner who had a small practice in town in addition to acting as their coroner. He'd asked just for the coroner. That meant someone was dead. Three terrible possibilities rose in his mind: Steven, Valerie or Ursula.

Logan recalled that Dr. Sullivan was to be transported today to Albany Medical and so he started at Owens and got lucky.

He found the doctor on the steps, leaving the front door of the funeral parlor. Dr. Brock Koutier was one of two county coroners and the one covering this half of the territory. The man wore practical clothes, rubber boots and a trench coat and carried a heavy shoulder satchel that he adjusted as Logan greeted him. In his late fifties with penetrating gray eyes and a hairline that teetered from receding to gone, his most notable feature was the thick graying mustache that would have been the pride of any buckaroo.

Logan relayed the message and then followed the doc to the Sullivans' home and found the county sheriff waiting for them in the yard. Trace shook hands with Koutier and then gave Logan a stiff handshake, pulling him in for a thump on the back. Sheriff Trace was also a vet and a former US marine. Fortunately, or unfortunately, he remembered all his time in the service and was haunted by different sorts of ghosts. Trace had comrades he could not save and once told Logan that he admired and envied him for having the chance to rescue three of the men in his unit.

Logan didn't know if he should be flattered by the warm greeting or annoyed at the abrupt ending of their call.

Blond, with broad shoulders and narrow hips, the sheriff carried himself with an air of authority that Logan admired.

"What's the situation, Trace?" asked the doctor.

"Mrs. Sullivan appears to have overdosed. Paramedics already called it on arrival. Just waiting for you to make it official."

Logan felt all the air go out of him. Dr. Sullivan's wife was dead?

"Who called it in?" asked Logan.

"Neighbor." He checked his notebook and read the name. "Freda Kubr."

"That's not her neighbor. Freda is Ursula's sister."

"Her sister is Freda Kubr?"

"Yes."

"I asked her to wait," said the sheriff. "But she was gone when I got here."

"Where is she?"

Trace shook his head.

"She was here last night," said Logan. "Where are the kids?"

"In school. I called and checked," said Trace.

"Do they know?" asked Logan.

"I'm not sure. Unlikely."

"Who got them up? Who got them to school?" Logan asked.

Trace had no answers.

Logan couldn't remember basic training, but he remembered the day Dr. Sullivan told him that he was an only child and that his wife had just her younger sibling. He had expressed sadness that his kids had no uncles or cousins or grandparents. Their only kin was Ursula's younger sister, unmarried, working at Hornbeck Central as principal Unger's office administrative assistant and now a village councillor.

"Freda works at the school. Did you call to see if she's there?"

"You call," said Trace. "Doc, come with me." Trace turned away. Logan kept talking.

"Freda was here last night, in this house. I saw her. She might even have spent the night here, gotten the kids to school and checked in on her sister after she got back."

"But why would she leave?" asked the doctor.

That didn't make sense.

"See if you can find her, Logan. If you do, ask her to call me. I need to speak with her, and I need to know if she will take custody of her niece and nephew." Trace rubbed his neck. "Those poor kids."

Doctor Koutier followed Trace into the Sullivan home. Logan dialed the school and was transferred to Mrs. Unger. He asked about Freda.

"I can't really say where she is. But she did take a personal day today."

"The Sullivan kids are there? She didn't take them?"

There was a pause. "Take them? Logan, what's going on?"

He told her the bad news. When he finished, Mrs. Unger spoke, her voice now exhibiting an uncharacteristic waver.

"She brought in the kids this morning. About an hour later she called me and said she needed a personal day. She sounded...panicky. I asked what was wrong and she said she was going out of town for a few days. She didn't tell me anything else, but if she already knew her sister was dead, how could she leave those kids?"

He didn't know. What he did know was that Freda would not have gone if she saw another way.

"She's running," said Logan.

"From what?"

"I wish I knew."

PAIGE DROVE TO Main and parked on the street in front of the constable's office at eleven but found the clock decal turned to tell visitors he would return at 1:00 p.m. Too early for lunch, she thought, but wondered where he might be.

The poster told visitors to call the state police in an emergency by dialing 911. But this wasn't an emergency. At least not yet.

She then made an uncharacteristic decision. She wasn't going back to work. She couldn't. Not until she had spoken to someone in law enforcement about the information she'd uncovered.

Logan found her a few moments later, standing before her locked car, fumbling in her bag for her key fob.

He pulled his truck behind hers and stepped out, greeting her and then drawing her out of the street and back to the sidewalk.

When he asked why she was there, the words tumbled out of her as if they were a waterfall. She babbled and raced until she reached the events of this morning and the missing computer and sudden new supervisor.

"Why not go to Lou Reber? He's your head of security down there," asked Logan as his worried eyes watched her.

"Because that is exactly what Ed would have done. If he found an irregularity or something that broke our security policies, he would have gone to his direct supervisor and to Lou."

"And now Ed's dead."

"Exactly!"

"We need Albritton. He's the investigating detective in charge of the Sullivan case." Logan spoke in a clear, measured cadence that she now found reassuring. "He's with the state police, and he needs to hear this."

Logan made two calls and then tucked away his phone.

"Found him. I'll drive. My truck's right here." He nodded to his vehicle behind hers,

"My car's probably faster." She pointed to the old gray Volvo sedan she'd bought used from a classmate during grad school. "You ride shotgun."

Before he had a chance to respond, she released the car locks and glided into the driver's seat. He stepped around to the passenger side and got in.

In a few seconds they were headed for the state police headquarters in Massena.

Outside Mill Creek he asked her to pull into a convenience store. She parked in a space directly before the doors, but he did not get out.

"Before we go further, I need to tell you something that happened this morning. The detective might know, too." He proceeded to inform her of Ursula's death.

Stunned by the news, Paige sat motionless, gripping the wheel with tight fists as if they were still underway, suddenly very glad they were not. Her mouth opened and then she closed it again. Her eyes teared and she blinked to clear them.

"It has to be accidental. She'd never... Oh, those poor kids."

He told her that Freda had left town without explanation. That news sent a shiver through her. Her hands dropped to her lap. Freda loved her sister. Yet, she'd left her niece and nephew after Ursula's death.

"She knows something. Whatever Ed told his wife, she probably told Freda."

Logan nodded. "Possibly."

She stared at the storefront, not really seeing anything as she groped for answers. All she knew was that the walls around her were closing in and she didn't know why.

"I'm afraid that giving this file to the state police could get me fired."

"That file might be the reason Dr. Sullivan is dead. You owe it to him to do as he asked."

Logan had such a clear moral compass. He wasn't afraid, never had been. That was probably why he was able to pull three wounded marines to safety under heavy fire.

Logan was a living reminder that there were drawbacks to bravery. She did not want to leave Lori orphaned, like the Sullivan children. She understood Freda's need to run because she was battling the same impulse.

"Want me to drive?" he asked.

enlist without even consulting her. Sound still confused him. But he worked successfully with kids as an assistant coach. Under supervision, she reminded herself.

Apprehension zipped through her. Here was Logan again rushing to her rescue, as he had done by reenlisting. Here they were preparing to become irrevocably involved in this investigation and possibly place herself and her family in danger. Paige stopped walking.

Logan was again ignoring self-preservation as he had done by reenlisting and by saving those men. But he did not have a daughter. Paige wondered if seeing Albritton was a terrible mistake and wondered, too, if she was a coward for her doubts.

Logan gave her an odd look. There was no doubt in his expression and no fear. She began moving again, knowing that if she didn't, she'd run all the way back to Hornbeck. He walked her up the road past the dying flares, reduced to small piles of gray ash, and the swirling lights of the trooper units. Logan spoke to the young female trooper who was directing traffic into a single lane. She radioed ahead and then told them that the detective was coming back to meet them.

Detective Albritton arrived a few minutes later in a trooper's uniform and the iconic flat-brimmed Stetson with the purple hatband. He was tall, in his midforties with a bristle of hair so short the color was impossible to determine. His sunglasses shielded his eyes, but deep lines flanking his mouth spoke of a man who performed a difficult job.

Logan introduced her and explained where she worked and that the man who had died yesterday in Hornbeck was her coworker. He did all that with hardly a missed word or hesitation.

She explained her relationship to Dr. Sullivan and the

"No. I'll drive." She got them back under
to the New York State Thruway, her mind racin
the vehicle.

Forty-three minutes later she pulled over at
marker 167, just shy of Exit 41 on the Northway. Ahea
her, the lights of several state police cars flashed agai
the gray afternoon. Her stomach churned with acid. Paig
flicked the key to the off position and placed both hands
on the wheel. They were so close, and yet, once again,
something was in their way, this time what looked to be
an accident up ahead. Logan exited and came around
to her side, giving her just enough time to reconsider
her convictions and wonder if she was making a terrible mistake.

Logan opened her door and offered a hand. She slipped
her palm against his, the feeling as natural as breathing.
Until their eyes met, and her heart took over, beating a
steadily increasing pace.

He isn't the same, she told herself. He doesn't remember. If she told him again about Lori, would he remem
ber this time? Logan no longer went to therapy. She ha
seen no more evidence of the early trouble he'd expe
enced with short-term memory. His recovery was c
plete, wasn't it?

Paige needed to speak to someone about this, hi
tors, she thought. She needed to hear from the
despite the gaps in his memory, he was now
of remembering and that she was not, again,
ing his condition or seeing only what she wis
She didn't want to do anything that would l
or endanger Lori. But would loving him rea
daughter at risk?

He was no longer impulsive. He liste
didn't think that this Logan would do sor

text message that she received, showing Albritton the message on her phone. He photographed the screen and then said he would be certain that Dr. Sullivan's watch was collected as evidence.

"Initial findings are accidental death. But this puts things in a different light. Did you happen to check his computer, as he directed?"

Paige told him that she had and that Dr. Sullivan's computer had since been removed and swapped with a new one for his replacement. She handed over one of the two copies of the file that she found most troubling.

Detective Albritton opened the page and read.

"So this document seems to be a letter Dr. Sullivan composed and addressed to Mr. Sinclair Park. Who is…?"

"Production manager at Rathburn-Bramley in Hornbeck. He is also Dr. Sullivan's direct superior. My position, a quality-assurance specialist, is to test the products. We work in conjunction with production to assure the safety, consistency and quality of each drug produced on site."

Albritton nodded and his gaze flicked back to the page. "Did Park receive this letter?"

"I don't know."

Albritton studied the paper copy. "Sullivan writes here that he has noted that samples from several batches of production have 'not been correctly logged and the oversight might result in some product going into the marketplace without all quality testing in place.'"

"That's correct."

"But you do not know if he sent this to Park via email or by paper copy."

"I do not," said Paige.

"Let's back up a minute, Dr. Morris. Doctor of what, exactly?"

"I have a doctorate in microbiology. I'm a processing microbiologist at Rathburn-Bramley."

"Meaning…"

"Basically, I check to be sure that our products are free from mircroorganism contaminations and that the finished product is sterile and free from corruption. We run routine collection and testing of raw material, samples and all final products. But according to this—" she pointed at the printout "—some product has been produced without adequate testing. Without any testing, really. That's what Dr. Sullivan is writing about."

"And because of the contents of this letter and the removal of Dr. Sullivan's computer you think…"

The detective was very good at open-ended questioning, she decided.

"I don't know, but it occurs to me that his death might not be accidental."

"You think this case might need to be moved from manslaughter to murder?"

"I just wanted you to be aware of this information." But in her heart, she was thinking, yes, it could be murder. They dealt in controlled substances, and even a casual observer knew that bad people made lots of money off the illicit drug trade. Had Ed inadvertently stumbled onto something related to that?

He tucked away the printout and her card in the inner pocket of his coat.

"I appreciate you two driving up to see me. You were on my list of callbacks, Dr. Morris. But as you can see, it has been a busy twenty-four hours."

Paige looked past the detective to the tow truck using a winch to drag a crumpled compact car from the ditch at the median. The roof had collapsed, the plastic fender hung and the hood had folded like a perversion of origami. She shuddered.

"I'll get back to you with any follow-up questions."

"Is there anyone else I should speak with?" she asked.

"Sheriff of the county is assisting in the investigation. His name is Axel Trace. Though he's stepping down end of the month. But I can assure you that I have received this evidence and will take appropriate actions, including getting Dr. Sullivan's computer, hopefully this afternoon."

"One more thing," said Logan and he told the detective about the untimely death of Mrs. Sullivan. The detective looked like a wolf catching the scent of prey. His eyes narrowed and his mouth twitched.

"I didn't know. That's very sad. Timing is suspect. I'll get in touch with the sheriff as soon as I finish here."

"Let me know if I can help," said Logan and extended his hand.

Logan and Albritton shook hands. He nodded at Paige and then returned the way he had come. Logan walked her back toward her car.

"I'm going to get fired," she said.

"That's against the law."

She gave him a look of skepticism and he had the decency to glance away. She was well aware that most whistle-blowers were fired and the rest were demoted, transferred or given poor evaluations.

"You did the right thing," said Logan. "Sometimes that comes at a cost."

She thought about the cost of Logan's doing the right thing. A Silver Star seemed a poor trade for all he had lost. But could he have done otherwise? Determined to do a worthwhile job while providing for the wife he planned to take, he'd served his country. Then he had saved the lives of three comrades and lost her. The rest had come back. He could walk. His speech was still improving. But the hearing cognition had not improved. And the memories… His father said the doctors thought those were gone forever.

Paige weighed again the costs of continuing to keep Lori's parentage from him. Initially, he had proven incapable of retaining the information. Now he was processing complicated details in relation to this case. There was no reason to delay. She needed to tell him again about Lori and this time, she was certain, he would retain the information. Should she also tell him about Lori's accident as a baby?

Was it now possible for them to try again?

She knew what her mother would think about that.

But now he had a job and he wasn't the joke that many thought. He was doing that job and she was proud of him.

On the walk to her vehicle, she thought about Logan's words and what they might mean for her. It was true she could lose her job, but she wouldn't be able to sleep at night knowing what she did. Knowing that her friend might have been murdered and that the culprit would get away with it. She would never have been able to keep silent.

When she got back to Hornbeck, she dropped Logan off at his office at just after one, just as the sign on his door had indicated. That coincidence made her shake her head.

At work she was greeted by Lou Reber, who told her that Dr. Sullivan's wife had overdosed the night before and had died. She told him that she had heard the news from the village constable.

"Grief is a funny thing," said Reber. "Depression, too.

People in that much pain just…well, it's too much sometimes, is all."

As far as she knew, Ursula was not depressed before Ed's death, and Paige couldn't imagine the woman abandoning her children, even as she suffered the loss of her husband. The fact that Reber had been so glib about it at first annoyed and then concerned her. Was he spinning her death to cover something up?

Paige headed upstairs to find Jeremy speaking with Dr. Sullivan's replacement.

Carol Newman arched her brows at Paige's appearance. "There you are. Is everything all right?"

"Personal business," muttered Paige.

Newman glanced at the wall clock for a long moment before returning her attention to Paige. "In the future, I'd prefer it if I were in the loop."

"Yes. Of course," said Paige. She collected the samples that awaited her. Throughout the rest of the day, she kept expecting someone from IT or security to arrive and escort her off. If they checked Sullivan's computer, they'd see that someone had logged in to the device after he had died and exactly what she had been doing. Surveillance footage would show them it had been her.

Maybe his computer was just sitting on a shelf somewhere, waiting to be wiped. If they wiped it, they would have no idea, except when the detective arrived to ask for it. Would he give them her name or would they have to figure it out with their own internal investigation?

"Paige?" Jeremy was watching her with his brow lowered over his eyes.

"Yes?"

"Did you hear what I said?" he asked.

She shook her head.

"They found the truck that killed Dr. Sullivan."

Chapter Eight

Paige had been so lost in her own troubles that she did not even hear Jeremy's revelations. Her coworker slid his stool closer to Paige before continuing.

"The truck belongs to a guy with a record for possession and a DUI. He's driving on a suspended license."

"Who?"

"Some guy from Plattsville Center," said Jeremy, referring to the small village to the northwest of them.

"What was he doing here?"

"That's all I know. The sheriff arrested him. Yazdi was down on the loading dock and heard it on the scanner," said Jeremy, referring to one of the senior custodians at the plant.

Their new supervisor meandered over to Paige, holding a clipboard out in her direction.

"Dr. Morris, are these your test results?"

Paige glanced at the data sheet as her stomach knotted. Those were the results of yesterday's testing, done after she had received news of Dr. Sullivan's death and his final text. Had she made some error?

"I'm afraid these numbers are incorrect," said Newman, confirming Paige's fears.

Paige looked at the data but saw everything within specifications.

"Calibration? There is no calibration data."

That couldn't be right. Paige glanced at the empty box on the top of the sheet beside Newman's extended index finger. She'd filled that in. Hadn't she? The preliminaries were a matter of routine. Done before each series.

She glanced to Jeremy, whose expression reflected worry to her shock.

"I'm sure I ran them."

"That may be so, but you did not record them. This entire series needs redoing."

"I'll get to that right now."

"No," said Newman. "Not you. Dr. Chen will cover it. I'm sorry to do this, but your absence earlier and this glaring mistake, I'm afraid I'll have to put this down in writing. Do you have any other reprimands in your record?"

"*Other* reprimands? No. I don't." This was sudden. Was Dr. Newman intent on discipline at any cost? Or was something else going on?

"Hmm." Her expression seemed skeptical.

"I can assure you, Dr. Newman, I am good at my job."

"All evidence to the contrary," she said.

"This is ridiculous."

Jeremy shook his head, warning her to back off.

"I did those tests and I recorded the data."

"Then how do you explain this?" asked Newman, waving the clipboard.

"I can't," she said firmly, as if daring the woman to contradict her.

"Yes. I see. You are denying that you failed to run the calibrations?"

"I am."

She nodded, made a note and then glanced up at her.

"I'm suspending you until further notice."

Paige shot to her feet. "What?" Could Newman even do that? Paige had such a stellar record under Ed, she hadn't ever had to bother keeping tabs on company policy regarding suspensions.

Newman was already on the phone requesting security. Paige gaped and blinked like a fish who suddenly found itself hooked and landed as security arrived. It was Tony Fitzpatrick, one of the newer guys who seemed to spend as much time lifting weights as he did at work. He was accompanied by Ken Booker, the head of human resources who relieved her of her security badge and keycard.

Paige had the humiliating experience of being walked out of the lab, flanked by the two men. The elevator ride seemed endless, but in the lobby she had the additional mortification of being trooped out past Veronica Vitale, the CFO, who paused from speaking to Lou Reber to watch her march past. Lou joined the procession. The three men did not leave her side until she was in her car. There Tony, Lou and Ken waited as she turned the ignition, set the vehicle in gear and drove out of the employee lot.

Her mind reeled, trying to comprehend what had just happened. It screamed setup. But was Newman responsible for it or someone else?

More immediate questions faced her. Where should she go? If she went home, her mother would interrogate her, and she just didn't feel capable of explaining right now.

Had she made that mistake or had someone doctored that form? But why would anyone do that?

The possibility that this was tied to a conspiracy did occur to her. But the more likely scenario was that the distraction of the text and the death of her supervisor had led her to make an oversight.

Even so, suspension seemed extreme, especially since she'd never made such a mistake before. All of yesterday's work would need to be repeated. She would be willing to stay late to do that. She vaguely wondered if she should call Newman and offer to do so.

Without realizing where she was going, she found her Volvo sedan parked before the constable's office on Main Street. Orange signs had been fixed to the light poles notifying the public that there would be no parking allowed tomorrow on the main street. The Harvest Festival, she realized. That meant tonight was the spaghetti dinner at the firehouse. She had planned to attend with her mother and daughter. Now she was so embarrassed. Having to face a lot of questions about work just made her stomach hurt. Paige put the sedan in Park and switched off the ignition. Then she folded her arms over the top of the steering wheel and lowered her head to her forearms.

Someone tapped on the glass of her side window.

She startled and turned to see Logan peering in at her. Paige opened the door and stepped into his arms. The familiar scent of him merged with the memories of the man he had been. His arms were still strong and his cheek was still rough.

He rubbed her back as his words rumbled through her with a deep, low vibration. "What's wrong, Paige?"

"I got suspended."

Logan drew back to study her face, cupping her chin in his warm hand. "Why?"

"They say that I made a mistake in testing. But I don't think I did."

"You can't prove a negative," he said and his hand dropped away.

She wrinkled her brow. "How do you know that?"

"I'm an officer of the law. It's a legal principle. And you told me. Once."

She had told him, but that had been in high school when Cliff Martin had been accused of stealing and denied he had done so. The missing phone had been found in his locker, so he was out for four days. Logan had pointed out that anyone who had that locker in the past years could know that combination and any of the administrators could have planted the phone.

She drew back and he resisted, then let her slip from his arms to perch on the edge of the car seat of her old Volvo, her feet resting on the pavement. Logan filled the space between the open door and the street as the occasional car rolled past them.

"You think someone is setting me up?"

"Possibly." He tucked her under his arm and led her back toward the office. There he veered to two plastic chairs, seating her in one and taking the other. He didn't have a desk so much as a counter, now used as a reception divider and for filling out paperwork.

"I don't know what to do," she said softly.

"You have to fight them, Paige."

"How? You just said that I can't prove I didn't do something."

He drew his arm from her shoulders, but she leaned against him and lowered her head to his chest. His arm came back around her and gave her a little squeeze.

"Did you hear they found the car that killed your boss?" he asked.

Paige nodded, feeling that her troubles were suddenly less important than the Sullivans'.

"Yes." She shifted, straightened and used the cuffs of her jacket to wipe her eyes. "Who is the driver?"

"State police made that arrest. It'll be in the news. All I know is that his name is Seth Coleman, he has priors and denies hitting Dr. Sullivan."

"Well, he would. Wouldn't he? Especially with his record."

"An innocent man would also deny it," said Logan. "He's the perfect suspect."

Too perfect, Paige wondered.

"They've removed Mrs. Sullivan's body."

"To the funeral home?"

He bobbed his head, his face grim.

"They're together again, I suppose," she said.

"No. Dr. Sullivan is in Albany awaiting autopsy."

Paige grimaced and lowered her head back to his shoulder.

He told her about Mrs. Sullivan's request last night to have the sheriff see her. "She seemed rattled when your plant's head of security showed up."

"Lou was there? That's odd. Isn't it? He's not a friend of the family."

Then Logan told her that he'd seen Reber coming down the stairs.

"Said he was using the bathroom."

"He might have been."

"Or he might have been taking some of the opiates you make at that plant and spiking something she would drink."

"That's a serious accusation," said Paige. "Kind of out there."

"Maybe. But a lot of this is out there."

"Besides, every single pill is accounted for. It's not like he could go down to the manufacturing floor and help himself." She rubbed her wrist with her thumb as she thought. Ed had mentioned some product, though, that seemed not to exist. Maybe not every pill was accounted for, after all. "Did you tell the sheriff this?"

"Yes. I told the sheriff that Mrs. Sullivan asked me to have him come see her today because her husband was worried about missing samples."

"Missing tests?" she asked.

"She said anomalies and missing samples."

Paige lifted her head. "I don't like any of this."

"Trace is listing the death as suspicious."

"This is terrible." Paige pressed her hand to her mouth, then dropped it.

Paige looked at him, really looked. He was leaner than in high school, having lost all the roundness in his face, leaving a hard jawline and cleft in his chin. His eyes were bright, and he needed a shave. She began to wonder if they could start again.

"Your speech has improved." Not only that. His ability to connect thoughts, to reason about what was happening. From what he'd just said, he might be ahead of the detective and sheriff on this case.

"Wasn't my speech. It was finding the words. They've been coming more quickly lately as if something in my head opened up the word bank."

"What about your memory?"

"Still gone. It's like during surgery. They give you that drug to knock you out, but it also makes you forget. Lose time. You know?"

Paige had never had surgery, but she was familiar with that drug as they produced it at Rathburn-Bramley.

"You remember how the anesthesiologist asks you to count backward and the next thing you know it's six hours later and you know you weren't out for six hours, but they are still all missing."

"Only for you it was five years."

"Yes."

"That must be very difficult." Was this really the first time they'd spoken of this? No, but it was likely the first time he could and would remember them speaking about it. She now realized how cold that might make her seem, and was filled with regret. She should have tried again, instead of doing as his family had requested and waiting so long.

"The hardest part is having everyone think I'm mentally challenged. You, too, Paige. Up until a few days ago you always looked at me with pity in those big blue eyes."

She glanced away. "I did. I'm sorry."

"I'm still in here. Missing time didn't change me."

"It did," she said, trying and failing to keep her resentment at bay, her anger at his rash decision to reenlist, at his family's request that she stop upsetting him with reminders of their past love. "You are not the boy who went away."

Not all the changes she noted were bad. He now seemed more prudent and less impulsive.

"That's what Connor says, too. Funny, though. I don't feel different."

The office phone rang, and Logan rose to answer it.

He said only two things. *I see* and *Yes*. Then he disconnected and turned toward her, his eyes sparkling and a smile lifting his features.

"That was Principal Unger. She says that child protective services can't get here until tomorrow and asked her to arrange suitable temporary placement for Valerie and Steven. She wants to temporarily place them with me."

"How do you feel about that?"

He gave her a sharp look. "You think I can't do it?"

She remembered the last time she had left a child in his care and the outcome that had changed everything again. But that was long ago, and the improvements were remarkable.

Was this the time to tell him how Lori got the scar on her chin or should she stick to giving him an answer to his question?

She deliberated all he'd overcome since his injury as she stared at the hard expression. He expected her to say she didn't believe him qualified. To her own surprise, she found that she did feel him capable.

"I think you can do anything you want to, Logan. If you want to take custody, you should do it."

He sat back and confusion tipped the corners of his mouth downward.

"Don't look so surprised, Logan. I've seen you with kids. You are a natural." She turned to a more difficult topic. "Do they know about their mom?"

"Yes. Unger told them. She asked the kids who they wanted to stay with, and Steven said he wanted me."

"I'm not surprised. You coach Steven. He idolizes you, you know?"

"Does he?"

She nodded. "Where are they?"

"The nurse's office at school. I'm going to get them now."

"I'll come with you."

Chapter Nine

Logan sat in the passenger side of Paige's five-year-old gray Volvo sedan heading for the school. She had rightly pointed out that, if she rode along, they could not safely drive two children in his pickup truck.

They parked right out front. School had let out thirty minutes ago and the buses had gone. They checked in at the main office and were walked across the empty hall to the nurse's suite.

Mrs. Warren had been the nurse at Central when they had both been in school, but Logan had never seen her this grim-faced.

Steven perked up at seeing Logan.

"Coach!" He shot to his feet. "Where's Aunt Freda?"

"Come on, sport," Logan said, drawing Steven under his arm and turning toward the door. There he paused, waiting for Paige and Valerie.

Valerie was on her feet and shifting from side to side.

Paige squatted before the girl, who was just shy of her twelfth birthday. Logan knew this because her father had mentioned they were taking her to Montreal to see the theater production of *Man of La Mancha*.

"Valerie, I'm Paige Morris."

Valerie glanced to her brother, already at the door beside Logan.

Logan knew that Dr. and Mrs. Sullivan hosted Dr. Sullivan's department party every July and had an annual Christmas party that Logan also attended. The kids always had a sitter for the winter gathering and headed for bed after making the rounds of the adult guests. But they were allowed to attend the summer event, so maybe they'd recall Paige.

Paige continued, her voice low and calm. "I've been to your house many times. Do you remember me?"

"You were on my team for Wiffle ball at the party," said Valerie. Her face was pale with worry and she glanced to her brother again before returning her attention to Paige. "You played first base."

"And you hit a home run," said Paige.

Happier times, thought Logan.

"Did they find Aunt Freda yet?" asked Valerie.

"Not yet." She extended her hand and Valerie took it, allowing Paige to walk with her past Mrs. Warren and out of the school behind Logan and her brother.

"Is she dead, too?" asked Valerie, her voice cracking.

"We don't think so."

"But she's missing," said Steven, asking the tough questions again.

Logan nodded.

Steven swallowed several times and then turned to Logan. "If they can't find Aunt Freda, where will we live?"

"With me and my dad for now. Is that all right with you?" asked Logan.

Steven nodded and bowed his head as the tears began to flow.

Logan recalled his mother's death when he was eleven years old. The suddenness and the randomness had struck him.

He had been in school the very next day. He remembered how the grief hit him in waves. Everything would be fine and then it wasn't. Then it would be okay and then the grief would leap on him all over again.

Would it be like that for the Sullivans?

"Harvest Festival tomorrow," said Logan. "You two want to go or skip it and stay with my dad?"

The two shared a long, silent moment that Logan could not interpret.

"If we go," said Steven to Valerie, "folks will stare at us and whisper. Or worse, they'll be really nice."

Valerie wrinkled her nose. A moment later she had her hands over her eyes as she wept.

Logan wrapped an arm around her. Steven was at his little sister's side, patting her shoulder.

"You don't have to go," he said.

"But I want to." Her words were muffled by her hands. "And I shouldn't want to."

"No, nonsense. You can go, Valerie, and have fun. It's okay. It doesn't mean you don't miss them."

She sniffed and nodded, but her head came up and she stared at the dark pines that lined the schoolyard.

"You'll go, then," said Logan. "Get some cotton candy and walk around. I have to work, but my dad can take you."

"I'll take them," said Paige. "You can join Lori and me. She'll be thrilled."

He gave her a grateful smile.

"And," she continued, "I'll bring you home anytime you want."

"*Our* home?" said Steven.

"Not yet. The police are still there," said Logan. These two kids did not deserve any of this.

"But not my mother?" asked Steven.

"She's not there."

"Then I don't want to go there. Not ever," said Steven. "I want to stay with you."

"That's what I want, too," said Logan to Steven. The boy finally looked at him, his astonishment followed by an assessing gaze.

"I do, Steven. I'd love to have you both stay with me."

PAIGE HAD BROUGHT Lori back home from the movie theater after eight. The animated feature had succeeded in entertaining Lori and in taking Paige's mind off her troubles for a time. An hour later, as she put Lori to bed, she faced the predictable questions, given all that had happened to her friends.

"Mom? What happens to me if you die?"

It was in that moment that Paige realized she did not have a will. She knew she needed one. But she was twenty-eight, and there always seemed to be time. What twenty-eight-year-old thinks of such things?

One who is a mother, she realized.

Paige wished she could tell her daughter that she didn't need to worry and that nothing would happen to her. But the Sullivans' tragedy showed that rare and terrible things did occur.

"If something happened to me, your grandmother would take care of you."

"What if it happened to both of you?" asked Lori. Her daughter's curling ash-brown hair framed her worried face and her golden-brown eyes seemed huge.

"Well, who would you want to live with?"

The answer was immediate and surprising. "Mr. Lynch."

"Connor or Logan?" she asked.

"Logan."

Paige blinked in shock. She had expected Lori to choose the parents of one of her classmates or her teacher or one of Paige's friends. Instead, she picked her father, though she didn't know him as such.

"Why Logan?"

"I like Logan. He's nice."

Paige didn't know what to say.

Her daughter went on with steady reason. Clearly, she had been thinking about this. "He's already taking care of Steven and Valerie. He has a job and he's a good coach."

And he's your father, Paige thought, but she said, "He is all those things."

She silently posed the question to herself. Who would she want to raise her daughter, if both she and her mother were gone?

The answer was immediate.

Logan.

"Let me think about it. Okay?"

"I'm going to ask him."

Paige's entire body went cold. "It's not done like that. I'd have to ask him."

"Will you?"

Paige used her index finger to lift Lori's chin and used her thumb to trace the jagged scar, white now and slightly raised, that threaded from her chin and across her jaw. "Sweetie, his brain was injured. I don't want to overburden him."

"But he's all better now."

When she spoke, her voice was sharper than she had intended as the worry rose up inside her.

"He's not," said Paige. *He's not because he doesn't remember us. And it's better that way, so I don't put weight on his shoulders he might not be ready to handle. But was he ready?*

For a long time Logan struggled to simply care for himself. But now… Had her young daughter identified what she had failed to notice? Logan was better or at least much improved. Perhaps now she could tell him what had been between them and, this time, he would remember. Connor certainly wouldn't like it.

Her daughter thumped the coverlet with her fists. "What about my real father?"

"What about him?"

"You never talk about him. When I ask, you just say he's out of the picture. Is he dead?"

"No."

"Then I want to meet him."

"That's complicated. He doesn't know about you."

"Then you need to tell him. Maybe he wants to be my daddy. I'm a good kid. He'd like me."

It was in that moment that Paige realized that while making her decision to keep Lori safe by keeping her daughter and Logan apart, she had robbed them both. She'd thought of this many times over the years, wrestling with what was the right thing to do. She'd grown so used to raising Lori on her own, was so careful to make sure she would not be hurt. What if she was misjudging his competence again? What if she told Logan and he fought for custody? Uncertainty gnawed. She couldn't bear that. But was Lori right? Was Logan capable of raising their child if the worst happened?

"I want to meet him, Mom."

All this time Paige thought she had been protecting her daughter. All this time she thought that she and her grandmother were enough. Why hadn't she known that Lori longed for a dad?

"I understand."

"Mom?"

"We'll talk about this some more later. Right now I need to sleep and so do you."

Lori lowered her chin, and Paige braced for a fight. But gradually her daughter released her clenched fists and finally nodded.

"Okay," said Lori.

She tucked her daughter into bed and smoothed the covers that she knew would be a wild tangle in the morning from her daughter's restless sleep. At the door she flicked off the light. The blue moonlight splashed through the window of Lori's bedroom, sending the shadows of the maple trees waving across the coverlet like the arms of skeletons.

"Good night, sweetheart," said Paige.

"'Night, Mom."

Lori looked like him, Paige thought, with her brown hair and amber eyes.

When she'd come home with a child, folks here did the math and assumed that she'd gotten in trouble in college after her breakup with Logan while he was deployed. No one knew he had been to see her before deployment or that their broken engagement had not stopped them from sleeping together before he shipped out. No one remembered but her.

She'd kept the truth from him to protect Lori. His dad had told her the doctors didn't expect Logan to survive his injuries, but he had. They prepared Mr. Lynch for the possibility that Logan would remain in a vegetative state. But he'd regained consciousness. They never expected him to recover the ability to speak, but he had. Back then it had been irresponsible of her to continue to try and make Logan remember them or to allow him any custody of Lori. When her daughter was a baby, Lori's injury convinced Paige that her daughter had needed protecting, but now she needed the truth. She needed her father. That meant that it was time for her to again tell Logan.

Chapter Ten

Logan was up at six and directing the food trucks and vendors to their positions on the Main Street. Setup began immediately as he worked to direct visitors' vehicles that began appearing a little after eight with traffic building until about ten-thirty. The volunteer fire department handled most of the parking and collected the five-dollar fee to fill Rathburn-Bramley's empty parking lot and the fields across Raquette Road. Mrs. Unger, the primary school principal and long-time member of the squad, was already there and setting up her crew. If any of them noticed the yellow caution tape at the head of Turax Hollow Road, they did not mention it. Dr. Sullivan's death didn't seem to be on the minds of visitors, if they'd noted it at all, and was momentarily set aside by the residents.

Logan went over to Mrs. Unger to see if she needed his help.

"No, we have it all under control, Logan. Thank you," said Unger.

He tipped his hat.

"Oh, Logan. I notified child protective services that you and your dad have accepted temporary placement."

"Great." He did not fail to notice that she had said that he *and* his dad had accepted placement as if he alone could not handle the job.

"It might just be a day or two."

"They're no problem."

Then he blurted out, "Mrs. Unger, do you think I could keep them?"

She cocked her head. "What's that now?"

"Steven and Valerie. Do you think I could be the foster parent?"

"You… Well, Freda would have custody."

"Assuming they can't find their aunt or she turns down custody."

"Well, you would have to be vetted and you're a single man and you have…issues." She shook her head. "I'm sorry, Logan, I'm just not sure."

"You think my TBI keeps me from being a good parent?"

"I know you'd be a fine parent. But we are talking about fostering someone else's children. It's a different question."

"I see." That was a polite no. She didn't think him capable or didn't think he'd gain approval from CPS.

He'd grown used to people underestimating him, but this still stung. He knew how to care for someone, and he could protect them, even love them, as if they were his own children.

She lifted one shoulder and her mouth twisted. Logan knew the expression. She was not optimistic. "Tell you what? Get the forms. They're online. Then we'll see."

Mrs. Unger took two backward steps, turned and hurried away.

He watched her go. He wondered if he might be better off in a place where he was not constantly being compared to who and how he was before. His intelligence was normal, and he was up and running in all other ways except the difficulty with sound. But he knew people who were deaf and were excellent parents. His memory loss seemed permanent, but it wasn't as if he'd forget where he put the kids and wander off.

Logan headed in the opposite direction. He had spotted his father, the Sullivan kids and the Morris family sitting at the bandstand watching the Delaware Dixieland Band. The group was so old that they left dust behind them on the stage, but the music was upbeat and joyful. He was gratified to see Steven and Valerie both smiling.

"Can you join us for lunch?" asked Paige.

Logan nodded and then turned to Steven. "Tacos, corn dog or pulled pork sliders?"

"Corn dog!" said Steven, his cares momentarily set aside.

"Tacos!" said Lori, bouncing in delight. Her grandmother, Beverly Morris, glanced toward the sky, drawing a long breath through flaring nostrils. As she exhaled, the warm air in her lungs collided with the chilly atmosphere, making her seem suddenly a fire-breathing dragon.

Mrs. Morris didn't like him. He wished he could remember why.

They all left the bandstand, and Lori skipped ahead and clasped Logan's gloved hand. Paige took ahold of Valerie's hand, and Steven, Mrs. Morris and his father followed along. Logan offered a greeting to everyone he knew, which turned out to be a lot of people. He saw their smiles drop as their attention moved from him to the orphaned kids behind him.

At the first food truck the kids moved to examine the images on the side of the vehicle and Paige stepped up beside him.

"How are they doing?" asked Paige.

"They had a rough night. I found them both in the bottom bunk this morning."

"I can only imagine how hard this must be for them," she said.

"I want to be their foster parent," he said and waited for Paige to tell him that he couldn't or shouldn't.

"I think you'd be a godsend to them both."

"You think I can do it?"

"I know you can."

Logan glowed with happiness. Paige thought he could do it. She, at least, believed in him.

"Logan, when you get off work this afternoon, could you come by the house? I need to speak to you about something." She sounded serious. Maybe it was about the Sullivan deaths.

"Sure."

His father had already secured two corn dogs and one chili dog. Delivering them to the Sullivan kids, the group moved to the taco truck. Their last stop was for pizza for Paige and sausage stromboli for him and his dad. Mrs. Morris professed not to be hungry.

They moved to the picnic tables he had helped erect this morning when the street had still glittered with frost.

His father set off to get them drinks and Paige went to retrieve some napkins. He watched Paige go and saw her pause to speak to his brother, Connor.

There was a loud sound and he turned to Steven.

"Fire truck?" he asked, looking about.

"Noon bells," said Steven. "At church."

Logan returned to his meal, pulling back the paper wrapping.

At the food truck, Paige reached for a stack of napkins and came face-to-face with Connor Lynch. She stifled a groan at being waylaid. Connor's thinning hair was trimmed short and he wore a dress shirt, tie and bomber jacket. As a Realtor, he was always looking for that next listing, searching for a professional but casual vibe that instead made him appear as if he were trying too hard to be cool.

"Nice of you to join my dad and brother."

"They're our neighbors."

"Still, I worry that Logan might misinterpret your kindness."

More like Connor had, she thought. "I'm not worried."

"I am. He's my brother, Paige. I know what he was and what he is. And I know that he is never going to be that boy again. But you're still waiting. It's like you are trapped. I want you to know that I'm here for you."

For the thousandth time she regretted going to prom with him. His senior dance had been a chance for her to join an event off-limits to most underclassmen and a real feather in her cap. But for Connor, it had been a demonstration of his affections. Her acceptance only encouraged his hope that she would become his steady girl. At the time she had not yet been dating Logan. But soon afterward she made her choice and Connor was still licking his wounds and looking for his chance. He was the one trapped in the past.

He'd tried again when Logan had come home to Walter Reed Hospital in Virginia and her visit had shown her how grievous his injuries really were. She wished that had been the last time. But clearly, he was not giving up. It had bothered her that he'd used his brother's injuries as an opening to her heart, but she had tried to understand that he'd been as upset as she'd been at Logan's hospitalization and long recovery.

"Logan is much better."

"Yeah, well enough to hand out comic books on fire safety to kids and work as an assistant coach. He's a big success."

Yet both the Sullivan kids and her daughter picked him to care for them.

Connor wasn't looking at her. He was looking at Logan. "Do you know he wants to be the Sullivan kids' foster dad?"

"He told me, yes."

"I hope you dissuaded him. The state will never approve him. A man, a soldier with a TBI?" His laugh was cruel.

She felt herself flush, but was it from indignation or shame? Was she a fool for hoping she and Logan could be the couple they once had been? Nothing could make her happier, but Connor's unkind reminder of Logan's limitations had brought her back to reality. Perhaps Logan didn't need to be burdened with more. He was already taking on a lot. And she would not place Lori in jeopardy again because of her refusal to accept that things had changed.

She admitted that she had a blind spot where Logan was concerned. But he was handling everything well, she thought. Her daughter, Lori, wanted to know her father. How would she feel when she learned it was Logan?

"Here, have some coffee," said Connor. "You look like you could use it." He handed over a cup.

Paige thanked him and then waved the napkins toward their table and her daughter's face, now smeared with taco sauce.

"Got to go."

"Paige," he said, delaying her, his tone turning more serious. "You must think about Lori needing a father. A capable, successful father, one with no…issues. If you do, I'm standing right here."

She didn't know what to say. He was essentially proposing to be with her for Lori's sake. Now her warmth turned to a simmer. What nerve! He was trying to use Lori, whom he rarely even spoke with, to soften her heart toward him. First he'd purchased that big house, the one he knew she loved and now this. She couldn't deal with this right now, not with everything else she was facing.

"Ah, Connor, I'm not… We're doing okay, Lori and I."

"You could do so much better," he snapped as he cast another glare at Logan and then turned away. She suppressed the desire to respond. How cruel of him to paint his brother as something "less than." And how rude to imply she would be settling for "less than" if she chose Logan. She tamped down her anger. She resolved to stay away from him.

Paige returned to the table, swabbed her daughter's face and drank the coffee with her cold pizza. The coffee was as bitter as her mood.

"What's wrong?" asked Logan.

"Who are we without our memories?"

"I don't know. But sometimes I think I'm better off not recalling the urban engagement in Iraq or the men who I didn't save. I think it's my brain's way of protecting me from some of the terribleness of war. The guys I saved, I met two of them, again and for the first time. One of them told me that he'd do just about anything to forget what happened."

She stared at him. Logan had forgotten the horrors he had seen in Iraq—a good thing. But in the process, he'd forgotten them, as well.

Chapter Eleven

Paige woke in the dancing morning sunlight with a pounding head in the twisted covers and discovered she was dressed in her jeans and undershirt, but had lost her coat, boots and sweater. Her hair was a wild tangle and her throat felt as if it were lined with fiberglass insulation. She blinked against the intrusion of light and hooded her brow with one hand. This was her bedroom but somehow, she had lost time.

There was a knock on her door.

"Yeah," she croaked.

Her mother creaked open the door a crack and peered in.

"Mom. What's going on?"

"That's what I'd like to know."

"How did I get here?"

"Don't you know?"

She shook her head and pressed one hand on each temple against the pounding.

"Connor Lynch brought you home last night around seven. You were slurring your words. How much did you drink last night?"

"Last night? I was at the Harvest Festival with you."

"Yes. But I took Lori back with me after you left and five hours later Connor Lynch brought you in. He said you headed over to the beer tent and he saw you needed some help getting home."

"That's impossible."

Her mother continued to grip the doorknob and stare at her with worried eyes.

"I know you are upset about being suspended."

"I am upset. But I wouldn't get drunk over it. I have a daughter."

"It is unlike you," agreed her mother.

"Where's Lori?"

"Playing in the yard with the Sullivan kids. Logan and his dad are watching over them. I didn't tell him about last night. I told him you were working on your résumé."

"It's a suspension, Mom. I'm not fired."

"Well…" Her mother made a vague gesture with her hand.

Paige flopped back down on the bed, her head splitting. She forced her eyes open. "Did Lori see me?"

Her mother nodded, and Paige groaned.

"I don't understand any of this."

"You were very upset. Screaming at Connor and at me. It took Connor ages to get you to settle down. You frightened Lori. Me, too, truth be told."

Why couldn't she remember any of it? There was just a huge blank place where yesterday should be. The yawning void terrified her.

"Connor said I should keep you home today. That he'd cover the damage at the Lunch Box."

The Lunch Box was the only eatery on Main, other than the upscale country inn. Had she been at the diner? And what *damage* was he talking about?

"And do his best to make amends at your work."

"Amends?"

"He said you threw a rock through one of the ground-floor windows at work and then took off. He found you thirty minutes later standing on a counter at the diner and kicking the condiments to the floor."

She squeezed her eyes shut.

"Also, one of the cakes and the glass cake stand." Her mother sighed, her expression disappointed. "You haven't been drunk like that since your sophomore year in high school. Remember?"

Connor had been there then, too. His senior prom and one of the worst nights of her life. She'd been drunk, but not drunk enough to do what he'd wanted.

"I wasn't drinking yesterday."

Her mother motioned to the nearly empty vodka bottle beside her bed.

The ringing of the front doorbell brought her mother around, and Paige groaned.

"Whoever it is, send them away," she managed through clenched teeth. Her stomach was churning as if the acid inside was set to the spin cycle.

Her mother's footsteps whispered out the door and down the stairs. A moment later the front door creaked open. Paige heard female voices but could not make out the words. The footsteps on the stairs made her brace. She'd told her mother that she did not want company.

"Paige, honey, the sheriff is here to see you."

LOGAN WATCHED THE county sheriff's mud-splattered SUV pull into the Morrises' driveway followed by two state police cruisers. He'd been in the yard playing catch with Steven, Lori and Valerie. The grass flowed from his father's property to the Morrises', broken only by the dirt drive leaving to the Morrises' detached garage.

He waved but Sheriff Trace had his head down and seemed in a hurry.

He called to the porch where his dad sat reading the paper. "Can you keep an eye on the kids, Dad?"

"Sure." His father glanced to the official vehicle in the Morris driveway. "What's up?"

"Not sure. Be right back," he said to Steven.

Lori fell in behind him and took his hand. He stopped and squatted before her.

"How about you let me go have a look."

Lori's worried gaze was on the house.

"What's happening?" said Lori.

"I'll go find out."

His father waved with the hand not gripping his paper and called Lori. She hesitated and then joined his father, the pair sitting on the porch in the love seat with the faded blue cushions, watching the lawmen approach her porch.

When Logan reached the Morrises' front door, he found it open. He called a hello and stepped inside. The last time he'd seen Paige was yesterday midday at the festival.

Paige had gotten angry after lunch. She'd said some hurtful things to him, including that he had never come back from Iraq. The comment had stung. He'd been surprised when she went off with Connor, leaving the kids with her mom and his dad. He tried not to be hurt, but he was still smarting over her comments. What did that even mean, *You never came back?*

They'd been having a nice morning at the festival and then Connor had shown up and she'd gotten as prickly as a porcupine. Seeing Connor with Paige was never easy, but yesterday was beyond challenging, with Paige laughing at Connor's stupid jokes and falling all over him. He'd been here all along, loving her since grade school. Wanting her for as long as he could remember and, then as now, never feeling good enough for her.

So why had he left her to Connor? Why had he joined the service and gone? Connor said it was because he couldn't stand to see him with Paige. But his father said that he and Paige had been serious enough to plan to marry, though he also said they had broken their engagement. Paige had plenty of time to choose and she had not married his older brother. As far as he knew, they hadn't dated since high school.

But if Connor wasn't good enough, then what chance did Logan have? Maybe she didn't want either of them.

Logan found the sheriff waiting in the front room, hands on his holster and eyes on the stairs. He gave Logan a proper salute, which Logan returned. In a different time and place, Logan would have been his superior, but that time had fled and Axel Trace was very much in charge.

"Everything all right?" asked Logan.

Trace shook his head. "I'm here to take Paige Morris into custody."

The shock hit Logan like a glass of cold water thrown in his face. "Why?"

"She's at the center of an internal investigation at her place of employment. They have reason to believe Paige has been stealing from the plant."

"Stealing what?"

"Drugs, they think. Opioids," said Trace. "I presented a search warrant to Mrs. Beverly Morris. We'll be searching the house and Paige's vehicle."

"She would not do this," said Logan.

"I sure hope you're right."

A female state police officer escorted Paige downstairs. Paige was dressed in boots, skinny jeans and an oversize white sweater. She wore no makeup and her hair was bunched up in a loose bun on her head. She looked hungover, with bloodshot eyes and a bleary, confused expression.

"Logan, will you sit with Paige while we execute the search warrant?"

"Sure," he said.

"Paige, you stay on this couch. If you don't, I'll have to arrest you. Do you understand?"

Paige nodded and sank down to the sofa as if she could not have remained standing if she had tried. Her face was blotchy with pink patches and her eyes watered.

Logan sat beside her, separated from Paige by the length of one couch cushion.

The trooper returned upstairs, appearing with Beverly a few moments later.

"What's going on?" asked Beverly.

Paige shook her head. "I don't know."

"She's searching your bedroom. She has a warrant. In my house! I'm calling our attorney." Beverly reversed course, heading, Logan assumed, for the phone in the kitchen, trailed by the female trooper. Beverly's heels clicked a rapid staccato as she disappeared.

"Paige, what are they looking for?" asked Logan.

"I don't know." She shifted to face him. "I don't remember anything since yesterday when you bought the kids corn dogs."

He narrowed his eyes on her. "That was twenty-four hours ago."

"I know!" Her voice squeaked.

"Paige, Sheriff Trace said your company is investigating you for theft."

"What! That's ridiculous."

"Is that why they suspended you?"

"Logan, I would never steal from them. For one thing,

it'd be stupid. They have security you would not believe. Plus, stealing is wrong, and I have a moral compass."

"Is there more to your suspension than what you told me?"

She gave him a long, hard stare. "Not that they told me, but…" She had suspicions.

Paige hesitated, not certain she should involve him. He was their constable, but this might be dangerous. What would happen to the Sullivan children if something happened to Logan? She thought of Dr. Sullivan and shivered."

"But what?" he asked.

"I'm not sure I should tell you."

"Because I'm too stupid to remember or because I never came back?" He repeated her words with cold fury.

"What are you talking about?"

If you didn't remember saying something, were you still responsible for your words and the hurt they caused? Logan thought so. "I don't know, but it's what you said to me yesterday afternoon before you told me to go get lost again."

"I never said that."

His fury dissolved into worry. He took her icy fingers in his hand. "You did, Paige."

She shook her head and burst into tears. "I don't remember."

And he knew exactly how terrifying that could be. Logan pulled her in and held her. "We'll figure it out."

"How?" she cried.

"Paige. I got you. But you have to tell me what is going on."

"I don't know what's happening. Dr. Sullivan's replacement said she was filing an official reprimand. That could get me fired."

"But not arrested," he said.

"I think something might be going on at work."

"What?"

"I don't know." Paige clasped her hands together and pressed them to her forehead. She closed her eyes and then spoke. "Dr. Sullivan found something, and he died. I'm not certain that was a coincidence. Then his wife committed suicide. And I'm wondering if Ursula really did that—took her life and left her two children without a soul in the world to care for them."

"And Freda fled."

"I hope she's all right. Why would she run like that, unless she was afraid?"

Or was she guilty? No, he didn't think that was true. Freda had no connection to the plant or anyone there outside the Sullivans. If Freda ran because she was scared, she obviously suspected someone had killed her sister and brother-in-law and those persons would stop at nothing to get away with their actions. He stared at Paige, his mind settling on a troublesome thought.

"They've chosen you as a scapegoat."

"Who has?"

"We have to figure that out."

"But the state police know about this. I filed a statement with Detective Albritton."

"Does the sheriff know that?"

She shook her head. "I don't know."

"You might be wrong about that file or you might be the only one who knows what's going on at your company."

"But then why is this all happening? All I know is that something was made and not tested. I have the batch numbers."

"It's enough." He lifted a brow and studied her. "And what about yesterday?"

"My mother tells me that your brother brought me home in the evening. She said that I was drunk and that I threw a rock through a window at my company. Also, I was the center of a disturbance at the Lunch Box."

"Doesn't sound like you. Not even drunk you."

"What does that mean?"

"I've seen you drunk, Paige. You get happy and then you get sleepy." He had her hand again. "You don't throw rocks. Come on." He dragged her to her feet.

"What are you doing?"

"Taking you to Glens Falls Hospital for a blood test. I think you were drugged."

"But Sheriff Trace said he'd arrest me if I left this spot."

"If you are right, they are going to arrest you anyway, Paige. We need to prove that you were drugged before whatever you took is out of your system. Now, come on."

Chapter Twelve

The blood was taken at Plattsville Medical Center, and the rape tests were negative. Whatever had happened to Paige yesterday did not include sexual assault.

She emerged from the ER to find Logan speaking to Sheriff Trace, who was taking notes in a notebook. He waved at her and tucked away the pad.

"Any results?" asked the sheriff.

"Not yet. They said they'd contact me."

"And me," said the sheriff. "Paige Morris, you are under arrest on suspicion of theft of company property and products, damaging company property and trafficking a controlled substance."

Paige managed only a strangled sound in her throat as her mouth gaped. What was he talking about?

"I haven't taken anything," she whispered.

"Paige, don't say anything else until we get you an attorney," said Logan.

"But I haven't done anything."

"You deny accessing a colleague's computer?"

She closed her mouth and kept it closed as the sheriff read Paige her rights and then escorted her out with Logan following beside them.

"When will she be charged?" Logan asked.

"Monday."

"Arraignment?"

"Monday, as well."

"Where?"

The sheriff gave him the address of the federal court in their county.

"You'll keep her safe until then?" he asked.

Trace nodded. "I will. I'm finishing out the month and then Kurt Rogers will be stepping in as sheriff. He's working with me now during the transition. That means we are not shorthanded for once. So one or the other of us will be with her until her arraignment."

"Can I post bail?"

"It's a felony charge, so no bail until arraignment."

Paige began to shake. This was really happening.

Logan said his goodbyes and promised to tell her mom where she was and what was happening.

Paige was escorted to the sheriff's SUV, placed in the back seat behind the Plexiglas and transported north. The rain that had been forecast arrived and immediately turned to a slushy mix, coating the grassy surfaces on the highway. Before they reached their destination, the salt and sanding trucks made the season's first appearance, splattering the windshield with their ice-melting mix.

Once at the Onutake County jail in Kinsley, New York, she was checked for warrants, photographed and finger-printed. After which, Paige sat in a plastic chair beside the sheriff's desk, despondently wiping the ink from her fingers with a wet wipe furnished by the sheriff.

Through the office doorway came a stocky man with close-cropped steel-gray hair and a white mustache that covered his upper lip. He wore a sheriff's uniform that fit snugly across his chest. He offered Paige a kind smile.

"Miss Morris, I've been looking forward to meeting you."

Sheriff Trace made introductions. "This is Kurt Rogers, my mentor and soon to be my replacement."

Paige was escorted through the door and the pleasant conversation ended when she found herself quickly placed in one of three cells. Sheriff Trace told her he had business and was leaving her with Rogers. She nodded mechanically, knowing she could not trust herself to speak. The tears were already brimming in her eyes, and the fear gripped her trachea and squeezed.

She glanced about the cramped surroundings. There was a stainless-steel sink and toilet. On the sink was a small cake of soap wrapped in paper and across the sink was a small white cotton face towel. The bunk was slightly smaller than twin size, with a metal frame, mattress with a plastic cover, and a blue blanket and sheets each in separate plastic wrappers. The walls were concrete, painted an unfortunate pink, the color of lobster bisque. Outside the cell in the corner was mounted a small camera, the red light's glow indicating that it was on.

A scraping sound brought her around and she found Sheriff Rogers placing a metal chair in the open doorway.

"Make yourself comfortable," said Rogers, motioning to the bed.

Comfortable was not how she was feeling. Lost. That was more the word. Bewildered. Shocked.

"Have a seat, Miss Morris."

She dropped onto the bunk, facing him.

"I'm not allowed to talk to you," she said.

"Yes. I know. Not about the matter at hand. But will you tell me about your company?"

She did, answering all his questions about what she did at the plant and what products the company produced, and which were manufactured in Hornbeck.

"So you make things with live viruses?"

She nodded.

"And a lot of gases?"

"Yes. Used in hospitals by anesthesiologists. Oral surgeons, as well, and some in the offices of other specialists."

"And narcotics?"

"We call them opiates. Narcotics are illegal."

"Yes," said Rogers, working his thumb and index finger over his mustache. "How do you know someone isn't skimming product away from the manufacturing floor?"

She explained the system of checks and balances, the accountability and record keeping.

"But you make up the batch numbers?"

"That would be Sinclair Park. He's in charge of production."

Rogers smiled. "This Park fellow, he in charge of all the drugs you make?"

"Pharmaceuticals."

"Right. He the guy?"

"Yes."

"Who supervises him?"

"He reports to the CFO and CEO of Rathburn-Bramley."

"Names?"

She told him that the CFO was Veronica Vitale and the CEO was Allen Drake.

"Your head of security is Louis Reber. That right?"

"Yes."

"And new hires?"

"My supervisor, the new product assurance director."

"Yes, because of the hit-and-run. We processed the man accused, Seth Coleman. He was arraigned and is in custody awaiting trial."

As he should be, she thought, and then realized she might soon face the same situation.

"Who do you report to now?" asked Rogers, now tipping precariously back in his chair so that it rocked on the hind two legs.

"Carol Newman, an outside hire and the one who suspended me. Now I have questions for you."

He answered them all. Yes, she could have visitors. Bail hearing would be at the same time as arraignment and Rogers thought her chances for bail were good.

"The sheriff was so quick and I didn't understand— process, I mean, all that he said. I'm being charged with theft and possession. Is that right?"

Rogers lifted a brow.

"The charge isn't for using, Paige, it's for trafficking. They found a bag with over 500 pills of oxycodone in your mother's home in your room."

Paige lifted the blanket, still wrapped in clear plastic, and hugged it to her chest.

"Impossible."

"If that's true, then I'd say someone wants you out of the way."

Chapter Thirteen

Her mother hired a criminal defense attorney out of Glens Falls. Alison Eckersley arrived early Monday morning. She had thick red hair pulled into a low ponytail, pale skin and gray eyes. Her ill-fitting suit was an unfortunate shade of brown and was not cut for a woman so well endowed, making it tight in the wrong places and baggy where it should have hugged.

Paige sat in the conference room of the jail with Ms. Eckersley after discovering that her arraignment was in ninety minutes. Eckersley explained that the charges were entirely drug related and that, if found guilty, the quantity of drugs found on her premises would constitute a class B felony that could land her in federal prison for eight to twenty years. Her defense attorney wanted to use lack of knowledge as her defense, claiming she did not know the drugs were on her premises. The problem with this was that the baggie in which the drugs were found was from her employer. Her lack of memory of what happened to her on Saturday night and into Sunday morning complicated her case.

She'd told the attorney all she could about the problems she had at work, Dr. Sullivan's text and her suspension on what she believed was either a mistake or a setup. Finally, she explained about filing a police report with Detective Albritton and receiving a blood test in Plattsville.

Eckersley's brow knit as she scribbled notes.

Paige's mother arrived twenty minutes prior to their departure to the arraignment, escorted by Sheriff Trace.

"Leaving in ten minutes, Counselor."

Her attorney waved him away.

Her mother looked a mess. Her makeup was uncharacteristically heavy-handed, her hair was flat and her eyes were red-rimmed.

She carried with her an envelope with Paige's blood work.

Paige scanned the report, which showed that she had in her bloodstream both opiates and Rohypnol.

"Rohypnol?" said Paige.

"What's that?" asked her mother.

Her attorney leaned in to look at the results.

"Roofies," said her attorney. "It's a date-rape drug sometimes used to treat insomnia."

"I didn't know you had insomnia," said her mother to Paige.

"I don't and I didn't take this."

"Knowingly," added her attorney. "We can use this in your defense."

"I would never take this," said Paige. "Someone slipped this to me."

Her mother sucked in a breath and then blew it away. Her hand was still pressed to her heart when she spoke. "Who?"

Her attorney glanced from Beverly to Paige. "Great question."

Paige's skin went cold as her body went into panic mode. She tried to rein in her fears and let the rational part of her mind sort out who and why.

Scapegoat, Logan had said. Some person or persons were setting her up. But who among her friends and family would help make her the fall guy for...what exactly?

One possibility emerged, but she pushed it away. He couldn't do this to her. Could he?

THE ARRAIGNMENT WAS FAST. Really, really fast. Besides the officials, the courtroom included her mother, Logan Lynch and Carol Newman, her new supervisor.

Paige did not speak. The prosecuting attorney laid out the evidence they had, including the opiates, stolen from her plant and found in Paige's bedroom after an anonymous tip was received by the state police. Equally troubling, the prosecution delivered a bank statement indicating that there had been a deposit yesterday of $11,000 into Paige's checking account. She was still reeling over that bombshell as her attorney denied all charges on her behalf and asserted that the charges were invalid and should be dismissed based on Paige's blood test results, but the judge deemed there was enough evidence for her to stand trial. Bail was set at $45,000. Her mother looked lost. They didn't have that kind of money.

Paige was escorted back to jail for lunch where Sheriff Rogers explained that, if her family did not post bail, she'd remain here in their custody until her trial, which was over a month away.

She wasn't hungry but forced down the chicken and biscuits, coffee and pumpkin pie. The dessert made her wonder if she'd be home for Thanksgiving or eating that meal here in this cell.

Sometime in the middle of the afternoon she received a visit from Detective Albritton.

He stood leaning on the locked door. "I went to the funeral home in Hornbeck to speak to the coroner. He had a list of all belongings found on Dr. Sullivan. They did not include a smart watch."

She thought for a minute. "There must be a record of the text somewhere."

"There is. I have it. Dr. Sullivan has three phones on his account. One for him. One for his wife and one for his son, Steven. He also has a smart watch linked to his phone. I requested the call and text data. It includes the location. His final text matches the area where Dr. Sullivan was struck and killed. It also matches his time of death."

"You think someone sent it after he was dead?"

"No, I think Sullivan sent it to you after he was hit and before he died. I think someone knows about that text and possibly the email you discovered, and that is why you are sitting here."

"You think I'm being set up."

He nodded. "You know, those watches have an interesting lock feature. They lock when they are removed from the wearer's wrist. Until then, anyone could have read that text or anything else."

"So they would have to have been at the scene?"

"Or in the ambulance or at the funeral home. I'd say the person who removed that watch checked it first. Then they would have known on Thursday that you received a text and what it said. If we are right, you have come to the attention of a person or persons willing to kill your supervisor."

"But he was hit by a guy with a record of DUI."

"He was hit by his vehicle. I've spoken to Seth Coleman. He denies driving his truck at the time, and I have to check his alibi."

"You think someone stole his truck and used it to kill Ed? Set him up, too?"

"I'm chasing that lead. I believe that whoever this is, they don't yet know that you spoke to me. And they would not have known that you went to the hospital until your attorney mentioned it at the arraignment. I got there late but noted who was in there. Logan, your mom and a woman in a suit."

"Carol Newman. She is Sullivan's replacement and the one who suspended me."

"And she is on her way back to report what happened here this morning."

Suddenly, Paige wondered if this cell might be the safest place for her.

The heavy metal fire door beyond the row of cells creaked open and Rogers grinned in at them.

"Bail's been posted. You, my dear, are free to go."

LOGAN WRAPPED THE dove-gray winter coat that had belonged to his mother around Paige's shoulders. Then he held the door to the station. She paused in the entrance, blinking up at the dazzling whiteness of the snow falling from the sky. In the twenty-four hours she had been in custody, the weather and the season had changed from fall to winter. The slush that had splattered against the window yesterday afternoon had blossomed into perfect feathery flakes of snow. The fluffy powder reached five inches.

He helped her into his truck. The drive back to Hornbeck was awkward, with him trying to think of something to say and her wiping her eyes with a crumpled napkin. At arriving at her home, she seemed to pull herself together.

He walked her toward the house.

"Could you come in for a minute? Maybe we could talk."

He glanced at his watch. "I've got to pick up the kids."

She nodded. "All right. Soon, though. Okay?"

He remembered her wanting to talk to him after the Harvest Festival, but they'd never had the chance.

"Is this about the investigation?"

She shook her head. "No, it's personal, Logan."

Now he didn't want to speak to her, as dreadful possibilities rose in his mind. Foremost was the 'it's not you, it's me' speech.

"Thank you for coming to get me," she said as they walked side by side in the snow. "I don't know how my mom managed bail when she can barely keep this house."

"Your mother? No, she doesn't know I bailed you out yet. I think she'll be surprised."

Not as surprised as Paige, who had stopped walking and now stood staring at him with one hand holding closed the top of his mother's gray woolen coat and the other flapping up and down as if she were attempting a one-armed takeoff.

"*You* posted my bail?" She stared at him as if he were a stranger.

"Yes."

"How did you… Oh, Logan, you didn't mortgage your dad's house or anything."

"No. I have savings. My military pay and most of my salary from the constable position. I've been saving for something, but I can't remember what. Maybe it was for this."

"You've been…"

"Saving."

Instead of the hug and kiss he'd been hoping for, Paige burst into tears. He wrapped his arms around her and pulled her in. She clung and sobbed.

"We'll get you through this, Paige. I'm here for you." As he comforted her, he didn't want to let go. She was so broken right now, so wronged. He had to help make things right for her. Paige, of all people, didn't deserve this.

"You've always been there. But I just didn't see it."

She pulled back and tipped her head so she could look up at him. They walked together to the porch that wrapped around the side of the farmhouse. At the top of the stairs she faced him, her cheeks pink and her eyes bloodshot. He paused at the bottom of the steps.

"Thank you for posting bail."

"You're welcome."

"You don't have to worry. I'll be making my appearances. You'll get your money back."

"Not what worries me."

He switched subjects. "Have you narrowed the list of people who had access to your food and drink on Saturday?"

"I've been thinking about it."

"Good."

Saturday, she had breakfast at home and then they headed to the festival.

"I was eating all sorts of things at the festival."

"Concentrate on the drinks. It is a pill that is tasteless and colorless in liquid, though some manufacturers are adding a blue center so it will show up in some clear beverages. What did you drink?"

"Hot cider from the apple orchard folks, a soda with lunch."

"Okay. Anything else?"

"Coffee." Paige sucked in a breath. The only thing she had drunk that was not from a vendor was a cup of coffee delivered to her by…Logan's brother, Connor.

"What?"

"Oh, Logan."

"Paige?" He grasped her elbow and guided her to a seat on the snowy step. "You've gone white."

She gripped his arm so tight that her fingers began to tingle. Then she saw spots. His hand went to her back and he pushed her forward so that her head was between her knees. She could see their footprints on the snow-covered step, wavering now as if she stared at them through water.

"Deep breaths," he instructed.

She gasped and pinched her eyes closed. The buzzing in her ears gradually receded. Paige opened one eye and then the other. Her vision was clear. Her fingertips no longer tingled.

"I think I'm all right," she said.

His hand drew away and he squatted before her, staring up at her with troubled eyes.

"You said you had coffee. Did someone give it to you? Who was it?" he asked.

"Connor."

Chapter Fourteen

Logan stood so fast he staggered back off the step and into the snow. When he regained his balance, his skin was clammy, and he felt sick to his stomach.

"He said you were drunk."

"If I was drinking, I don't remember it. I do remember him bringing me a cup of hot coffee. He also brought me home. Mom told me that I was so drunk, Connor needed to help me upstairs." She placed a hand over her mouth and stared at him with wide eyes.

Logan absorbed this stomach punch. "He was upstairs."

She nodded frantically.

"Was he alone up there?"

"I don't remember any of it."

Logan headed into the living room and asked Mrs. Morris the question. Had his older brother been upstairs alone at any point?

"Yes. He asked me to go get her some water. I went downstairs to get the glass and fill it."

"How long was he alone?"

"I went right to the kitchen, but then, there was mud all over the floor from where they'd come in. I mopped that up. Maybe ten minutes."

Long enough to plant whatever was necessary in Paige's bedroom, Logan realized.

His big brother was a village councilman, one of the few Realtors in the area, and his business had boomed when Rathburn-Bramley had built their manufacturing plant just down the hill, bringing new employees to the area who all needed housing.

Could it be possible that he had done this to Paige? Logan didn't want to believe it. But the evidence pointed directly at his brother.

It was the hardest thing Logan had ever done, but instead of rushing over to confront Connor, he called Sheriff Trace.

"Logan. What's up?" asked Trace.

He told him of Paige's suspicions.

"She's accusing your town councilman, who is your older brother, of drugging her?"

"She is. But I also witnessed her drinking a soda from one of the food trucks and having a glass of cider from a local orchard." He prayed that anyone other than his brother had done this.

"Do you know of any reason Connor would do such a thing?" asked Trace.

"I don't. I am just making you aware. My brother gave her a coffee. She drank it. Shortly afterwards she became confrontational, which is unlike her. Then she left our group and later that evening, Connor brought her home and carried her upstairs."

"So he also had access to Paige's room."

"Yes."

"Was he alone with her there?"

"According to her mother, yes again."

"I agree with Paige. This does not look good for Connor. I will ask you not to mention this conversation to him or confront him. You have an obvious conflict of interest and, if Paige is correct, to do so could further endanger her."

That possibility had not occurred to Logan.

"I don't think I can pretend that I'm not suspicious."

"I'm looking into this now. Give me until tomorrow. Then you can be there when I question him."

"All right." But he wondered if he'd be able to keep from accusing Connor until then. If he did this, Logan needed to know why. Why set up a woman he professed to care for? Was he tangled up with the people who had killed Dr. Sullivan?

Logan's anger shifted to worry. Were the people who had killed Dr. Sullivan threatening his brother?

PAIGE TUCKED HER daughter into bed later than usual. It was a school night and it had been after nine before Paige had even thought to ask if Lori had finished her homework. She hadn't and so they had sat together working on a language arts worksheet on punctuation before turning to her daily math assignment, measuring units. Cups to pints to quarts and before they were finished, Paige really wished the country had made the switch to the metric system.

Her weariness seeped through her bones, and it was a struggle just to climb the bedroom stairs. Her mother had gone to bed over an hour ago, but her television still yakked away, the bluish light flickering under the bedroom door. Paige steered Lori into the bathroom. Her daughter emerged a few minutes later in her pajamas. The sky-blue fleece was covered with polar bears and penguins in ski hats. Paige tucked her in and left the hall light on, as always, before heading to her room on the other side of the hall at the front of the house. This was the smallest room and the only one that did not have access to the flat roof over the porch. Both her daughter and mother could climb out their window to that roof and walk to the back of the house where the grade of the property made it only a five-foot drop to the ground. Because of this, her father had long ago placed an escape ladder under Paige's bed in case of fire. Her father, a volunteer with the local department, knew something about fires.

Once in bed she tossed and turned and finally got up to check on Lori to find her on her laptop. She closed the device and took it with her to her bedroom.

Lori appeared twenty minutes later and asked to sleep with her. Paige threw back the covers and her daughter slipped beneath the coverlet. Tucked in, safe and warm, they dozed in her big full-size bed until the acrid smell of smoke woke them.

LOGAN WOKE TO the sound of applause as if he were at a concert with many people cheering and clapping. He was already reaching for his trousers.

"Logan?" his father shouted.

"Yeah." He sat up and threw the covers off in one motion. His heart began pumping at the alarm he heard in his father's voice. "Someone is pounding on our door." There was a pause and then his father shouting again. "It's two o'clock in the morning!"

Logan burrowed into an old sweatshirt and stood to tug on his trousers. At the bureau, he shoved his bare feet into his boots and stooped to tie the laces. As he left his room, he passed his father, whose room was on the opposite side of the staircase. His dad had his robe on over his traditional pale blue pajamas and was cinching the sash on the cranberry-colored terry robe as Logan passed him.

"Who the devil?" said his father.

Logan thundered down the stairs as the knocking continued. He saw a small figure beyond the glass. He opened the front door inward. Beyond the storm door, Mrs. Morris stood on his welcome mat in her bathrobe and bare feet.

He didn't need to ask what was wrong. The snow reflected the orange blaze of the Morrises' house. He stepped out and across the porch so he could see. The entire second floor was blazing, and black smoke billowed upward as snow continued to fall from above.

"Dad! Call the fire department! The Morrises' house is on fire!" He grabbed Mrs. Morris's shoulders. "Where's Paige and Lori?"

"I don't know. Inside. I think they're still inside!"

He leaped from the porch and out into the snowy yard.

It took an eternity to run through the seven inches of accumulation and cross the hundred and fifty yards that separated the two houses. He reached the porch and found the front door open. The draw of air sucked past him and up the stairs, fueling the fire above. He made it halfway up to find a wall of flames filling the upper hall. Smoke billowed outward through the opening where the window should have been.

"Paige!" he shouted. The flames roared, stealing his voice, consuming the dry wood of the two-hundred-year-old structure.

He pulled his sweatshirt up over his head and tried to reach the landing, but was forced back by the heat.

Retreating out of the house, he went for the aluminum ladder in the Morrises' shed. Running, staggering and slipping as he tried to find traction in the slippery snow.

How long until the flames reached her? How long until the fire stole from him the only woman he had ever loved?

PAIGE CHOKED ON the thick smoke. The room was dark but there was an orange glow beneath her bedroom door. The smell of burning was all around, in every scalding breath.

"Lori!" She shook her daughter. To her horror, her daughter jostled from her shove and then remained still as death.

The carbon monoxide in the smoke—had it killed her daughter?

Paige pressed a hand to her daughter's chest and lowered her ear to her lips. The faint rise and fall accompanied the shallow release of air.

The smoke billowed, so thick she could no longer see the door.

"Mom! Mom! Fire!" Why hadn't the smoke detectors alerted them? She changed the batteries every spring at daylight savings.

Later, her brain instructed. Right now she needed to get them out. She wrapped Lori like a burrito in the bedding and pushed her to the floor. Then she crawled on hands and knees to the door, placing a hand on the antique glass handle. Reflexively, she jerked her hand backward before her brain registered the branding heat of the knob.

"Mom! Fire!" Smoke filled her lungs and she coughed and choked.

There would be no escape that way. Opening the door would release that deadly heat into the room. Paige retreated, crawling back until she hit the box spring with her head. Then she slithered on the floor toward her daughter.

The air was so hot. Her eyes streamed with tears. Choking, she tried and failed to call to Lori. Where was she?

Groping as she crept along, she realized that she was

dizzy. The air was leaving the room. Her lungs burned with each scalding breath. She reached out and felt the bedding.

Fists clenched on the blankets encircling her daughter as she dragged Lori toward the windows. Was she going in the right direction or was she heading back toward the door?

Her shoulder struck the desk, telling her where she was. Releasing her daughter, Paige rose. The smoke was so much worse. Just a few feet higher and the air was scalding. Her face felt as if she had stuck it into a preheated oven. Dry heat sizzled as she flipped the latches and opened the window. Fresh air, sweet and cold doused the heat, driving it back. Paige inhaled as the bedroom door blasted open and flames exploded through the gap.

She squatted, groping for Lori and finding her, dragging her to her chest and up onto the window.

"Paige!" The male voice came from somewhere below her. The smoke now poured past her and out the window. She could not see.

"Paige, drop Lori! I'll catch her!"

"Logan?" She tried to call his name, but the smoke turned her words into a scratching, crackling thing and she burst into fits of coughing.

She heaved until Lori hung half out the window.

"Are you there?" she called and could not hear her own voice.

Catch her, Logan. Save our girl.

She pushed, and Lori fell free, tumbling out into space.

"I got her!"

Paige smiled and crumpled to the floor.

Chapter Fifteen

Logan held Lori's inert body as he reached the foot of the ladder. His father had arrived and took the girl as Logan returned up the extension ladder.

"Is she breathing?" he called as he ascended.

"Yes," said his dad. "Hurry!"

Paige had been alive a moment ago. His feet clanged on each flat metal rung as he ascended toward the window that now billowed with thick smoke.

The black hole gaped, like the mouth of a dragon. He could see nothing within but the flames dancing like streamers across the ceiling.

He grasped the ledge and pulled himself into the dragon's jaws. The floor was so hot, he felt the wide painted panels of the wood peeling under his hands. He groped and found her, lying still on the smoking floor. He dragged her to him by her limp arm.

"Paige!" He choked. The air was too hot to breathe. He scuttled backward to the window. There was a current of hot air pouring past them on its way out and into the sky.

He had to get her out. He stood in the heat that burned his skin and lifted her out the window.

"Here, son! I'm here."

Logan turned toward the voice. His father, his fifty-four-year old father, whom Logan thought too old to be on a ladder, was standing below the window, taking Paige from his arms.

"Come on," shouted his dad. "Out! Grab the ladder."

Logan went headfirst out the window, hanging on the back of the rungs just above his father who stood on the front side of the ladder holding Paige in his arms.

The fresh air filled his lungs and he sucked in a breath.

His father struggled down, holding Paige over one shoulder like a firefighter.

A howling sound grew louder and louder, sounding like an opera soprano stuck on a high note. He glanced around to try and place the noise. Was that the fire?

Logan looked back to the window. Flames poured out of the hole and reached up to the roof. The side of the building was black with soot and he could not believe anyone had escaped that fire. Bright red lights flashed across the white blistering paint as the singer grew louder. The fire engines, he realized, looking to the road and the approaching emergency vehicles.

Logan scrambled down the back rungs of the ladder and climbed around the side, coming to the front half of the ladder and proceeding down.

His father reached the ground and crumpled into the snow, still holding Paige.

"You're on fire!" shouted Mrs. Morris, stepping forward to pat frantically at his shoulders. Logan dropped and rolled in the snow, hearing the hiss of extinguishing embers. The smell of burned hair caused him to feel his head. He felt nothing burned away and so scrambled to Paige. Mrs. Morris had dragged her granddaughter beneath the large maples that stood witness to the human tragedy playing out below them.

She hurried back to Lori and sat in the snow, tucking her bare feet within the bedding and bringing Lori into her arms.

Lori cried, curling into the arms of her grandmother. Logan turned to his father, who sat panting in the snow beside Paige, who was motionless.

Logan dropped to his knees beside her. He pushed her singed hair back and looked at the blackened, soot-streaked face. The tracks of her tears cut lines in the ash. She blinked up at him, her blue eyes wide with wonder.

"I'm alive."

Logan was nodding, unable to speak past the tears that choked him.

"Lori?"

"With your mom. Both okay."

"Miracle," she whispered, and then closed her eyes as her body went slack.

THE MORRIS FAMILY was transported to Mill Creek Medical Center for treatment by the Hornbeck volunteer fire department in the new EMS vehicle purchased by Rathburn-Bramley for the village. Paige was treated for smoke inhalation, scorched nasal passages and had first degree burns on her hand where she had touched the doorknob. That touch had likely saved her life, along with the help of her mother, who had run for help, Logan and his father, who arrived moments before the fire breeched the door, and the volunteers who had transported her and her daughter.

Lori had carbon monoxide poisoning and was on oxygen overnight in the emergency room. This facility was small, with only ninety beds, and all of them were currently occupied. Paige and Lori slept on gurneys in the same ER examination room, side by side, their oxygen flowing into the uncomfortable clear plastic masks.

Sometime very late in the evening, they were moved to a room. Lori barely roused, but Paige took the opportunity to shower before putting on a fresh hospital gown. Despite the scrubbing, she still smelled faintly of wood smoke and ash.

In the morning the oxygen was removed, and their breathing checked. A short time later they had a visit from volunteers from the American Red Cross. They had bathroom kits for both her and Lori, and a pink stuffed rabbit for her daughter. Lori clung to the bunny with a fierceness that worried Paige. Her child was growing past the age where such toys held her interest, but if anyone deserved the plush comfort of a stuffed animal, it was Lori.

They were also given bags of clean, new clothing and underwear. Lori was furnished with brown corduroy pants, bright purple fuzzy socks, new snow boots, a turtleneck, fleece jacket and snow coat, all in shades of pink and purple. Seeing the unfamiliar clothing laid out on her daughter's hospital bed only brought home to Paige that they had likely lost every personal possession in the upstairs area. The grief was lightened only by the realization that they were both alive.

Paige took the contact information from a volunteer who, before departing, assured her that they had plenty of donated clothing and household items and could help with temporary housing.

"Where will we live now, Mama?" asked Lori.

Where indeed.

"Let's check with Grandma on that one. All right?"

Lori's eyes held worry and her neck was still streaked with soot.

"Would you like a shower?"

Lori's face brightened as she nodded.

Rabbit stayed behind on the hospital bed as Paige helped her daughter get her shower going, handing in the tiny shampoo, body wash and conditioner bottles. As Lori washed, Paige cleaned up in the sink, using the hand soap, comb, toothbrush and lotion.

She left Lori in the bathroom to towel off and brush up, while Paige found a nurse, borrowed a pair of scissors, then snipped away the singed hair. Then she explored her bag of clothing. Paige found she had blue jeans, a tailored white blouse and a soft, fuzzy forest green sweater with a crew neck. The boots were tight but new. She loosened the laces and tried on the tan-colored leather jacket. She'd never owned a leather coat before, especially one that was so stylish and fitted. The loose buttons and general wear told her this was a donated item. As a result, the jacket was well broken in and she was grateful.

Lori appeared from the bathroom with her hand on the waistband of her pants.

"They're too big," she said, holding them up with one hand.

The problem was fixed shortly after breakfast, which they both devoured. Their nurse supplied them with several safety pins and Paige made the adjustment to her daughter's waistband.

It was nearly lunchtime when they were finally released. When they reached the lobby it was to find Logan waiting just past the reception area. His attire, unlaced boots, charred sweatshirt and mud-streaked trousers, indicated that he had spent the night on the waiting room couch. There was a white gauze bandage on his left forearm.

"What happened?" asked Paige.

"In all the excitement, I didn't realize I cut myself somehow. Needed staples to keep me from leaking."

"Oh, no. How many?"

"Thirty or so."

She blinked at that. "And you're all right?"

"Never better," he said. "New clothing?"

She glanced down at the unfamiliar attire. "Hmm. Yes."

"I like the leather jacket."

"I don't suppose there is anything left of our…"

He shook his head, his smile now tight. "I'm so glad that you and Lori are all right."

There was a long and weighty pause as Paige considered what might have happened and how blessed she was to have Logan there for her. He'd risked everything to reach them.

"Thank you, Logan, for saving our lives."

Logan gave her that dear, hopeful smile. She stroked his cheek and leaned in, kissing him tenderly on the lips. The contact was meant as an expression of thanks, but the instant her mouth touched his, the internal fireworks exploded, and her circuitry went haywire.

When she drew back, he was blushing and her daughter was staring up at her, slack-jawed.

Paige glanced from Logan to Lori and discovered her daughter's lip trembling, though whether from what she had just witnessed or at the magnitude of their escape, Paige did not know. Lori lunged toward Logan, wrapping her arms about his waist, trapping Rabbit between them as she buried her face in his side and wept. Logan cradled her in one arm, giving her narrow shoulders first a squeeze and then a pat.

Paige felt a lump, as spiny as the coat of a hedgehog, now lodged in her throat. Breathing past the obstruction, she took several small gasps as she reined in her emotions at seeing Logan hug his daughter. It was impossible. The fire and their escape and Logan being there every single time she needed him all crashed down on her. She stepped to his opposite side and draped her arms about his neck. His free arm drew her closer, and she let the tears fall.

She'd meant to tell him the truth about Lori the afternoon of the Harvest Festival. But then she'd been drugged and framed and sent to jail for a night. She had to tell him, but not here in this impersonal waiting room.

He didn't hurry them or draw back in embarrassment at this public display. He let them shatter and then slowly draw the broken bits back together again, knitting them into a new whole.

Paige drew away first and then Lori lifted her tear-smudged face and stepped beside her mother.

"Ready to go home?" asked Logan.

Only they had no home. Paige would have wept again if she had any tears left. Instead, she gave a nod. Logan swept a hand toward the exit and then followed them out through the sleet to his old truck. All three squeezed into the front seat, with Lori between them. Logan set them in motion.

"Where's Grandma?" she asked, now buckled in and peering out at the slush that slapped against the windshield like wet mud.

"She's at our house calling the insurance company. Said to tell you she'll be there or at your place seeing what to salvage."

"How bad is it?" asked Paige.

"Took the second floor and attic before they got the fire out. I expect the bottom floor will have heavy water damage."

Temperatures were dropping. The sleet was turning to snow. Soon all that water would freeze solid.

On the drive back, Paige began to wonder if she had underestimated Logan. Was he so different from the boy to whom she had given her heart?

Yes. He was. But in some ways, he was better. Kinder and more responsible. This Logan would not leave her or Lori to go off to reenlist. This Logan would stay and raise his child instead of sending money back from overseas.

"You all right, Paige?" asked Logan. "You're awful quiet."

"A difficult time, Logan."

"I'm here to help you. My pa, too."

"All my stuff is gone," said Lori, gripping Rabbit. "My trophies and my horse models. Everything."

"Things aren't important, Lori."

"I know. People are," she said, repeating the words she had heard many times. "But I still like my things, my bed and the bedroom curtains."

"We have our lives. It's a blessing," said Paige, wrapping an arm around Lori's shoulders.

"But where are we going to live?"

That stopped Paige. She drew a breath, held it and then pursed her lips and blew.

"You and your mom and grandmother are staying at our place. Your grandmother will have my mom's sewing room. You and Valerie will have my brother's old room and your mother will take my room."

Paige was shocked at the tingle that went through her at this revelation.

"Where will you sleep?" she asked, innocent of the possibility that she and Logan might share a bed, the bed they had shared nine years ago, in fact.

She glanced to Logan, expecting him to turn and give her a knowing look or wink. But instead he held his grin and kept both hands on the wheel. He never even looked at her as he spoke.

"I'll bunk with Steven and my dad in his room."

It hit her again. He didn't remember. This time the anger at his decision to reenlist, which had led to his brain injury and loss of memory, didn't surface. In its place, there was a deep, yawning sorrow.

"I can't put you out of your room," said Paige.

Now he turned, brows raised in speculation. "No?"

"I'll sleep on the sofa downstairs," she said and watched the speculation turn to disappointment as his gaze flicked back to the road. The snow was falling in earnest now, coating the grassy surfaces and sticking to the branches of the trees. Only the oaks held their leaves now. The rest of the trees stood bare and skeletal in the torrent.

"You can sleep with me and Valerie," said Lori, her voice holding a coaxing, hopeful tone.

"Sounds good, sweetheart." Then a thought struck her. "That's a lot of people, Logan. A lot of beds."

"Red Cross is helping with that."

"You know, I still have lots of toys and board games and books. So many books," said Logan to Lori. "I guess I used to be a big reader."

"Not anymore?" asked Lori.

"Letters jump around a bit. I can read, but it's not yet a pleasure. Getting better, though."

"That's because of the bomb that went off?" she asked.

"There wasn't a bomb. They tell me that I got hit right here." He pointed to the scar that threaded along his hairline to the side of his temple. The scar was still raised but it was no longer pink. "Part of the ceiling fell on me."

"But you saved everyone?"

"You know they never told me that. Just that I..." His

voice changed as if he were reading from a report. "Engaged insurgents while simultaneously evacuating three wounded marines under fire."

"Engaged?" asked Lori.

"That means they shot at us and I shot back."

"Did you kill anyone?" asked Lori.

"That's not the sort of question you ask, Lori," said Paige.

"It's all right," he said to her and then glanced to Lori. "Answer is, I have no idea. I was a soldier, so probably."

They reached Hornbeck and drove through the village and finally reached their house. Past the bare branches of the three maple trees stood what had been their home.

The entire top floor was charred black. The front windows were all gone and the exterior was burned down through the clapboard siding. The first-floor paint had peeled and the smoke discoloration made the paint seem brown in places. Pink insulation disgorged from between blackened two-by-fours spilled out onto the charred porch roof. Through the empty space where the windows had been, exposed electrical wires hung from what remained of the interior ceiling.

Logan pulled to a stop and the three went quiet. Paige stared at the yawning black hole that had been her window.

"How did you get us out?"

"That," he said, pointing at the sooty aluminum ladder that had twisted in the heat.

Thousands of tiny icicles glittered from the charred sides of the second floor.

Lori nestled close to her mother as she stared.

They had been so fixed on the house or what remained of it that they did not at first see her mother standing on the porch of the Lynch home motioning to them.

Logan pointed. "Your mom wants us."

He continued past her home and into his driveway.

Paige was not even out of the truck when her mother hurried down the stairs wrapped in an unfamiliar woman's coat that Paige suspected had once belonged to Logan's mother.

"The fire inspector wants you to call him."

Chapter Sixteen

Paige had come home from the hospital, wanting only to stretch out on her bed and sleep. But she didn't have a bed. The scorched and blackened box spring she had spotted on arrival in the yard beneath her vacant window told her that much.

Her mother wanted them to go over to the house to see what they could salvage. The walk between the houses showed Paige again how ferocious the fire had been. There was a pile of charred debris that might have been dragged out by the volunteer firefighter. She wasn't sure how else it might have landed in a heap below her window.

"What's that?" asked her mother, pointing.

Paige glanced from the rubble to the strands of yellow caution tape wrapped around the porch rails and across the side steps like a dubious garland. Upon reaching the bottom step they paused to read the notice affixed to both the closest porch beam and the front door. On the bright yellow post was printed in black:

DO NOT ENTER
CRIME SCENE

Below that was a white post with red lettering:

DO NOT ENTER
UNSAFE TO OCCUPY

THEY RETREATED TO the Lynch home. Her mother had been on the phone all afternoon, trying to reach the fire inspector and get answers as to who exactly had forbidden her to enter her own home.

Paige checked in at work and was informed she had an employment hearing scheduled for Friday at 9:00 a.m. sharp. She was advised to bring her attorney.

She barely remembered eating supper and was so dead on her feet that both she and Lori went up to bed at just after seven.

The next day she gave Lori the choice of school or a day off and her daughter, the social butterfly, chose school. In the Lynch's kitchen she found her mother, still in her robe, chatting with Mr. Lynch over their mugs of coffee at the breakfast table as Steven sat between them, shoveling breakfast cereal into his mouth.

Her mother glanced at Paige, who was now dressed in a borrowed pair of men's flannel pajama pants and an overly large US Marine Corps T-shirt.

"You look like you're off to boot camp," she said and took her coffee and the paper past Paige to the dining room. Paige watched her mother go, wondering if she was expected to follow. The smell of freshly brewing coffee convinced her to stay.

"Help yourself?" said Mr. Lynch, seeing the object of her desires.

"Thanks. Smells wonderful." Then to the boy she said, "Good morning, Steven."

His reply was garbled. She headed to the appropriate cabinet and retrieved a mug. Paige had been in the house often enough to know where everything was kept.

Mr. Lynch poured and motioned to the sugar and carton of milk on the table. From above, she heard the not-so-tiny feet charging up and down the upstairs hallway.

"Uh-oh. The girls are up," said Mr. Lynch and retrieved a six-pack of blueberry muffins from the refrigerator with the butter dish. He set the butter on the kitchen table with the breakfast cereal and milk. Steven took his bowl to the sink and headed upstairs.

"Where's Logan?" asked Paige.

"Went in to work early. The fire, I think," said Mr. Lynch.

Paige looked toward the back door. A melancholy too great to name turned bitter in her mouth.

"He's getting better, I think. Speech is improved. Not stuttering or groping around for words," he said.

"He can't process loud sounds."

"That's true. And the memory, well, it's gone, Paige."

She met his steady, sympathetic gaze.

"I know that, Mr. Lynch."

"Do you? Because it seems you are still waiting for him to show up."

She glanced away. "Don't be silly."

"It's not silly. I felt that way for a time. But now, instead of mourning the man he was, I'm celebrating the man that he is."

Paige frowned at that, thinking how wise and impossible that advice really was. How could she not want what they had shared? If only she remembered, did that make it less real? She felt her throat going tight with the pain of loss. It was so hard to grieve someone who was right here with you. Didn't any of them understand?

"Paige, honey. His heart remembers even if his mind forgets."

That broke the last of her control. Tears streamed down her cheeks.

"He just needs a little push, Paige. He knows he's not the man who was engaged to you. He's told me he doesn't think he's good enough now."

"That's not true."

"Truth and belief are different things. So, I'm afraid if you are waiting for him to do it, it will just not happen. It's got to be you."

"Do you think he'll remember this time if we tell him?"

"He's been retaining things perfectly. I think his doctors would be shocked."

"I think so, too."

"Time to tell him again, Paige."

There was a yip and shout from the girls upstairs.

He glanced toward the ceiling. "And past time for Lori to know I'm her grandfather."

The sound of pounding feet on the stairs preceded the girls' appearance. Paige snatched up her napkin and dabbed at her eyes.

Lori flounced into the room, joyful as a butterfly. She was dressed in her only outfit and holding her new rabbit in a headlock as she entered the kitchen.

"Good morning, sunshine!" Mr. Lynch said with exuberance that seemed as natural as breathing.

Paige swallowed hard and then crushed her napkin under the table in her lap. She turned to her daughter and Lori gave her an assessing look that lasted just longer than normal. Paige forced a tentative smile.

"Good morning, honey."

Lori's smile returned.

"Cereal or blueberry muffin?" asked Mr. Lynch.

Lori chose the muffin. Valerie appeared, making that two blueberry muffins. Mr. Lynch went to work as Paige sipped her coffee, forcing the hot liquid past the stubborn lump. It felt normal eating in the Lynch home. She couldn't remember how many meals she'd had here over the years but this house, she realized, was as close to a second home as one could hope for.

Mr. Lynch gave all three of them two halves of the toasted muffins that he'd browned in butter over a hot griddle. Their breakfast was served with orange juice and Lori finished first. When her mother offered to walk the children to school, Paige gratefully accepted.

Only after her mom, daughter and the Sullivan kids had disappeared did Mr. Lynch drop his smile.

"Logan thinks that fire was set. The inspector isn't allowed to say, but I get the feeling he agrees. Mighty suspicious, your boss, his wife and your suspension. Then this fire."

"What are you suggesting?" asked Paige.

"We need to circle the wagons. Something bad is happening here, and Logan is the man to keep you and your gal safe. But you are the one who needs to figure out what's going on, Paige."

She agreed with that.

"You need to use that brain of yours to figure out who is doing this and why."

She knew why. Those tests that were missing. The batches of unknown product. What were they, where were they and who was making them?

The house phone rang, and Mr. Lynch took the call, hanging up after a short conversation. Then he faced her again.

"Fire inspector is on his way. Wants to interview you."

Her stomach cramped, sending the muffin and coffee sloshing about her insides. If she had learned anything in the past week it was that things were not what they seemed, and being innocent was no protection from harm.

The fire inspector arrived just after noon, and Mr. Lynch ushered him in. After leading the way to the kitchen, he left them alone and the interview commenced.

She judged the inspector, Fulton Frick, to be in his midforties. He had prematurely gray hair the color of steel wool that bristled an even quarter inch from his head. His face was long, his mouth grim, and his nose twitched like a ferret catching the scent of a baby bunny.

After introductions, which included presenting his card, he withdrew a legal pad and a tape recorder.

"Do I have your permission to record this interview?"

Alarm bells sounded. He wasn't law enforcement, exactly, but still…

Sensing her hesitation, his smile reassured. "It will help with my investigation. Get your insurance claims settled faster."

"All right." Had she just said yes?

Frick switched on the recorder. At first, the questions were simple and the inspector's attitude sympathetic.

But within the course of twenty minutes, the questions he asked Paige went from easy to pointed with accusatory overtones.

"Did you remove anything from the home prior to the fire?"

"Like what?"

"Valuables, guns, jewelry, that sort of thing?"

"No. How would I have even known to do that?" She answered her own question. Someone setting a fire would know and might remove things that were too precious to lose.

"Would you be willing to let me have a look inside your vehicles, outbuildings and so forth?"

"Why?"

"Just part of the investigation."

"I don't think so."

"Do you have any online retail accounts?"

"Yes."

"Have you sold anything of value recently?"

"No!" Did she sound defensive or angry?

Did this guy really think she would burn down her own home?

Because he was acting exactly as if he thought she had burned down their house.

"You have smoke detectors."

"Of course."

"How many?"

"Three."

"Locations?"

She told him and he nodded, jotting her answer on the pad he had before him.

"We found three."

Paige shifted in her seat and glanced longingly out the window at the light snow that fell, covering everything in a pristine coat of white. What would the fire inspector do if she just got up, went outside and made a snow angel?

"And you say that the kerosene can is yours?" Frick waited with his ballpoint pen raised over the yellow legal pad. In the front pocket of his dress shirt sat an open pack of cigarettes. At first, Paige had thought that funny. Now she didn't find a single thing about him funny.

Frick might be just as deadly as the house fire, and threatened her just as surely.

"I said that we had one that looked like that in the garage."

He added to his notes and flipped to the next page. "How full would you say it was?"

"I don't know. We used it when we went camping last summer at Schroon Lake."

"And you have recently lost your job?" he asked, pen poised again.

Where had he heard that? "I did not lose it."

"How would you characterize your status, then?"

"Suspended." And then arrested and charged with corporate theft. If they made that stick, she would never get another job. In just under a week her life had fallen off the rails. Everything was out of control.

More scribbling.

"Would you say you are depressed?"

"No!"

"Have you considered harming yourself or others?"

Behind her the swinging door to the dining room opened. She stiffened, fearing that her mother had already returned early from picking up the girls at school, even though she knew this was dance class day. She didn't want her mother or daughter to hear any of this. The entire line of questioning was humiliating.

She turned to see it was not her mother, her daughter, the Sullivan kids or Mr. Lynch, who had left for his Tuesday afternoon bowling league. It was Logan standing in the entrance. He stood with one hand pressed to the swinging door. His expression was thunderous, and his eyes were fixed on Frick.

Chapter Seventeen

"Time for you to go," Logan said to the fire inspector.

Frick stood and switched off his digital recorder and dropped it into his coat pocket. Then he collected his notebook. Logan stepped aside and motioned toward the door.

"I'll be back," said Frick, his words seeming more threat than promise.

Frick headed out the kitchen door, his footsteps loud on the porch steps. A moment later she saw him out the window, venturing across the yard, leaving footprints in the newest layer of snow.

The sun glowed, a white sphere of light strong enough to break through the gray clouds that enveloped them. It was only midafternoon but already the sun dipped just above the tops of the tall pines to the west of the Lynches' yard. Daylight savings was just over a week ago, but she still had not adjusted to it being fully dark before five in the afternoon.

Logan stepped up beside her at the window.

"Thank you for that," she said.

"What?"

"For defending me." She stepped closer, so close that she could see each coarse hair in the eyebrows that sank low over his intent eyes.

"You're welcome."

"He doesn't think the fire was accidental, does he?"

"Seems not," said Logan.

"I didn't set that fire," she said.

"Paige, I know that." The smile he gave her radiated confidence. Then his smile faded.

"What?"

"I wanted to tell you yesterday, but you were so exhausted. It's about Connor."

She stiffened and her arms came up to fold protectively before her.

"I called Sheriff Trace and told him your suspicions about the coffee. I gave him the details and he's investigating."

He'd reported his brother. Believed her without speaking to Connor. The trust and the protection he offered her touched her heart.

"That must have been difficult."

He nodded. "It was."

Her arms dropped to her sides as she stepped closer. "Thank you."

He lifted a hand and cradled her chin on his index finger.

She craved that touch, couldn't do without it for even one moment longer. She took hold of his hand and pressed his palm to her cheek, closing her eyes to savor the rough texture against her skin.

When she opened her eyes, it was to see his expression had changed from concern to heat. She knew that look, had seen it reflected in the eyes of his younger self. Back then, just a glance or a touch could set them aflame.

"Paige?" he said, his voice now deeper, almost a growl.

"Will you kiss me again, Logan?"

He slid his hand through her hair, cupping the back

of her head as he angled for the meeting of their lips. The contact thrilled her with an electric charge of heat. A flood of memories washed over her, of a time when she had been younger and more trusting, believing that Logan would serve his country and come home safely to her.

She stepped forward, needing the pressure of his body against hers and lifting onto her toes to deepen the kiss. He drew her in, intensifying the contact of their mouths. Her tongue darted along his lips, and he opened for her. How had she survived all these empty days and nights without this?

Why had she denied them? It was all the same, exactly as it had been. Perfect. Strong. Unstoppable. His mind might have lost her, but his body remembered.

The heart remembers. The words danced through her mind as her skin turned to gooseflesh.

She stepped back, needing to look into his eyes. What if their kiss had sparked that place in his mind that had been damaged, those connections that stored their history together? She had to see. Had to know if he remembered them.

Logan struggled to keep her against him and then, seeming to realize she sought release, he let her go, moving her to arm's length and stared down at her in wonder.

"Wow," he said.

She could see the desire flashing in his warm brown eyes and the hopeful smile that curled his wet lips. His skin flushed and his pupils dilated. Was that recollection or need?

"Paige?"

She knew what his question meant. He wanted her. As much as she wanted him. She was tired of waiting, tired of being careful not to move too fast or repeat past mistakes. His father said she needed to make the first move and she wanted to take back some of what they'd both lost.

"Let's go upstairs," she whispered.

Yes, upstairs. Back to his bed and his life. She wanted him inside her, beside her, making her feel as only he could make her feel. Whole, wanted, needed.

She extended her hand, and they took the stairs at a run. Her mother was at dance class with Lori on Tuesdays, and Valerie was now joining them. Her brother was at basketball practice, and Logan's father would be picking him up after his bowling league. They'd all be gone until at least five. She and Logan had time, precious time together and alone.

Down the hall, they hurried into his bedroom where he paused to throw the lock. She had removed her new tight boots and yanked away the socks before he even turned. When he did, it was to find her tugging off her jeans and kicking them away.

"Are you sure about this?" he asked.

In answer, she threw her discarded sweater at his head. He caught it easily and then dropped it. Then he tugged his shirt and fleece pullover off in one motion. Her gaze flicked to the bandage on his left arm.

"It's fine," he assured her.

She released the bottom button of her blouse, her fingers fumbling and clumsy with haste.

He now wore only his jeans, which were unfastened to reveal a tempting line of hair that threaded south from his navel and into the tight denim.

"Let me," he said, stepping forward on bare feet. He began at the top of her blouse, opening each button and planting warm kisses along the naked flesh he exposed. She'd been dressed in a thick sweater and blouse and so had not bothered this morning with a bra. As he opened the two edges of the gaping fabric, there was nothing between his warm mouth and her skin.

The sound in his throat was a low hum of pleasure as he moved down to her navel and then back up. When he straightened, it was to smile down at her.

"Are you using protection?"

She nodded. Fool me once, she thought, having been on the pill since Lori's birth.

"I have condoms. I'll use one if you like."

The offer to protect her made her smile. He had not always been so careful.

"All right," she said, accepting his suggestion.

He moved to the drawer in his bedside table and then returned, offering her a small green packet that squished between her fingers.

"Will you do it?"

She smiled. "Love to."

He slipped back the edges of her blouse so that the fabric slid over her shoulders, but instead of removing the garment, he bunched the fabric in his fists, drawing her shoulders together and lifting her breasts as she arched. He draped her over his arm and kissed her breasts, starting at the outer orbs and moving toward the peaked nipples, with such excruciating slowness that by the time his mouth finally took hold and sucked, she was nearly mindless with wanting. She panted as he pressed more tightly to her aching breasts.

He walked her backward until her legs contacted the side of his bed. Then he lifted his mouth long enough to draw her blouse away and strip out of all his remaining clothing.

She glanced downward to find him ready and wanting; the sight was inspiration she did not need, and she fell back upon the bed. He knelt beside her, kissing and licking over her breasts and down to her navel. He looped his index fingers under her panties and dragged them away. Logan followed their descent with his mouth, his tongue giving her a hint of what might be in store for her.

The panties dropped away, and Logan paused to cast her a long look that she believed was appreciation.

"You are more beautiful than I ever imagined."

She smiled as he returned to his ministrations but something about his words bothered her. *Imagined*.

He was kissing her inner thigh now and she could not quite focus.

Ever imagined. Why was that wrong?

And then his mouth moved higher and Paige lost the power of critical thought. Logan was here with her again.

Chapter Eighteen

Logan lay on his back beside Paige with his arm around her shoulders. She rested on her side, nestled up against him, her hair a riot of curls fanning across his chest. He used his free hand to wind one of those curls about his finger, enjoying the satin of the strands and the heavy lethargy that filled him up like warm honey. She was warm honey, melting over him and around him. Taking him in and holding him tight as they both shattered. He'd brought her to her pleasure with his mouth and then again, this time together. He closed his eyes, remembering, as if he could ever forget.

Why had it taken so long?

Was it because he still lived with his dad?

He could have gotten a place of his own. But then he'd be farther away from Paige. He wouldn't be able to walk her home from her work at night. And he would not have been there to answer the door when their house caught fire.

She and Lori would have died. That thought terrified him. Whether she knew it or not, Paige was his anchor. He just never expected her to come back to him. No longer felt he deserved someone as smart and perfect as Paige. If being her neighbor was all he could have, he would have taken it. But now, he hoped for so much more.

He wondered if she knew he still loved her or if she thought this was merely about need. He'd have to tell her. Risk her laughing in his face and tell her that he was madly in love with her. That he knew that she was too good for him, but he couldn't help wanting her.

Ever since his injury, he'd become acutely aware of his imperfections and always felt people were measuring him up, judging his competency. It shattered him to consider Paige might think him incapable of loving her because when he was with her, he felt whole again.

Logan kissed her forehead, and Paige sighed, nestling closer. She threaded her fingers through his wiry chest hair, her index finger circling his nipple.

He sucked in a breath and she chuckled, the sound as sexy as the woman herself. He glanced at the bedside clock and sighed, squeezing his eyes closed in denial. Their private time was up.

"They'll all be home soon."

Now the sound emitting from her throat was half growl and half groan. She opened her eyes and smiled at him.

He released the curl he had collected. Then he used his thumb to stroke the velvety softness of her cheek. The feathery lashes lifted as her gaze met his.

"Did you say that I was prettier than you *imagined*?" she asked.

"I said more beautiful."

"Than you imagined?"

He smiled and nodded.

She pressed her hand to her forehead and rolled away, sitting on the edge of the bed, her drooping shoulders rounded.

"What's wrong?" He came up to a sitting position behind her.

Paige ignored the slicing ache in her chest as she stooped to retrieve her discarded panties and jeans. She stood to slip them on and then snatched her blouse from the floor, shrugging into the sleeves. Then she turned to him, her blouse unbuttoned. His gaze snapped to the skin visible between her breasts and down to the waistband of the jeans that she now fastened. When his gaze finally drifted up to meet hers, she saw appreciation and hunger reflected there.

He lay on his side, propped up on his good arm, the covers tangled about his middle to reveal his long, muscular legs, dusted with dark hair, the tempting stomach and well-defined chest, and now she was thinking of pulling off her jeans again.

"Everything okay?" he asked, those heavy, dark brows lifting over speculative eyes.

And she did not know who she should be angry at—fate for throwing them into this situation, or herself for expecting a man who had suffered a brain injury to magically heal himself.

His dad said that she had to make the first move. She surely had done that. There would be no turning back now.

"I have to tell you something." She slumped to the foot of the bed, out of easy reach. She tucked one foot up under her thigh and hugged her ankle for support. Despite her attempts to meet his gaze, she kept her attention on the white gauze bandage circling his injured forearm and then slipping lower to his hand now bunching the sheets as he pressed up to sit against the headboard. Properly braced, he spoke again.

"All right. What is it?"

She did look at him now, at the earnest, open expression and the worry. She'd done that to him and now wondered how much of this forced separation was her fault? Had she waited too long? She had tried to remind him of their relationship and of his daughter so often, and failed, that she'd nearly lost hope. Her dad said it was time, confirming her conviction. And Logan's actions spoke as loud as her heart. He could protect her and Lori. He was brave and kind and dear. He'd saved her life. He'd saved their daughter's life. He could love them, remember them, at least from here forward.

But his brain was damaged. He wasn't the same. And she'd had it drummed into her by his family that he needed to heal, he needed space, time, freedom to come back to some sort of normalcy. The real question was could *they* be the same?

Her heart was hammering now, with fear and hope. They could be. She could make them the same. She let herself entertain the possibility of a new beginning. It was that or keep their past forever locked away in her heart.

She shook her head, rejecting that choice.

"You're scaring me, Paige. What's going on?"

She dragged in a breath through her nose as she had once done on the high dive platform before taking her very first dive from the three-meter board. Then as now, there had been this same jackhammering of her heart and the buzzing in her ears as the fear and the thrill blended. A moment later she was safe, gliding through the deep blue water and back to the anchor of the aluminum ladder.

"You don't remember this, but…" She had made the approach. The three steps to reach the end of the board. Now came the commitment. The jump then the landing on the board. After that nothing could stop her from falling through space. "But you and I were engaged."

His smile was tentative, and his eyes were melancholy. "I know, Paige. Everyone told me that."

"You asked me out right after Connor's senior prom."

She looked away from the confusion on his face, gathering her courage. Was that guilt twitching inside her? Guilt at not trying to tell him what was his right to know? At giving up after repeated failures. Logan wouldn't have given up. He wouldn't have listened to doctors or his family. Nothing would have kept him from her. She needed to be more like him.

This was harder than she had thought it would be.

"We were serious, Logan. Steadies in high school and then I went off to college at Plattsburg and you went to Basic. But you visited me on leave and before the Military Combat Training. Five days in April. You visited again in July before sophomore year. That was when you asked me to marry you."

His eyes went wide. "I wish I remembered that."

She gripped his hand. "I wish that, too."

The joy in his eyes made her heart ache. He didn't know it all yet. He might not be so elated when he knew.

"Why didn't we get married?" he asked.

"We planned the wedding for the summer after I graduated. You deployed to Iraq and I worried. But you made it through all right. Then four days before Christmas, my junior year—"

"Your dad died," said Logan. His jaw was tense, and the muscles bulged as he clamped his teeth down on the final word.

The lump grew again. "You remember?"

"My brother told me. He said the dentist office closed and that you and your mom had struggled. Bankruptcy, he said."

"Yes. I almost quit school. Neither of us knew that dad used a home equity loan to finance my education. It was one of those loans with an increasing interest rate. And he still had student loans for medical school and for setting up his dental practice. The cars were leased. There was credit card debt. We only just saved the house. You were home for a little over a year working for a trucking company. I had no money for tuition, and I wanted to postpone the wedding. You wanted to get more loans to pay for my tuition and the wedding. I couldn't let you. Not after seeing what that debt did to Mom. I told you no, but you found another way. You reenlisted. I was so angry. I didn't take the money you offered and, I'm sorry, Logan."

"Why would I do that?"

"You wanted to be a hero. My hero. When I told you that I believed, still believe that major life choices like reenlistment and a combat assignment need to be discussed—"

"Of course."

"You were so angry that you asked for your ring back." His jaw dropped.

"It was a really difficult time. It felt like the whole world was coming down on me and then you had to report for duty and were gone again."

"*I* called it off?"

"Yes." Paige drew a breath as she jumped and then left the high platform. There was no turning back now.

"There's more. You left in August and you visited me at college before your second deployment and…" Paige hurried on as if trying for the smooth entry, hands braced, ready to strike the water, to get the words past the lump growing, by the second, in her throat.

"And…" he prompted.

This was the hardest part, the part she had felt she just could not do again, telling him and watching the shock, which was always followed by tears and condemnation that she had kept this from him. After all that, he'd forget her and Lori all over again. It seemed so pointless, cruel even, to tell him again and again. She prayed that this time he'd hold on to her words, this conversation.

Inches from entry now, the water in that huge pool rushed at her.

"We had unprotected sex."

His eyes rolled up and she could almost hear him calculating, counting. He drew his hand away.

"I found out I was pregnant in September—"

"She's mine," he said, interrupting.

"What?"

"Lori is my daughter."

This time she saw two things that were different from all the previous occasions when she had told him this. First, he'd figured it out without her telling him directly and second there were no tears. Now his eyes blazed and his mouth was set in a grim line.

She studied his gaze, trying to see if he recalled or if he had just made the obvious conclusion as she waited for the coming condemnation. She'd suffered it before. She knew she'd survive it.

"Yes."

His breath flowed away in a whoosh as if she had punched him right in the stomach. He crossed his arms over his middle, hunching forward as if he might be ill.

His voice was a whisper, but loud as artillery fire in the silent room. "How could you not tell me that I had a daughter?"

She landed on her stomach in a metaphorical belly flop in the deep end, the pain real as his eyes blazed with fury.

"I did tell you. I told you in September before you deployed. Connor and I visited you at Walter Reed in April of the next year, after your injury. You didn't know us. I was seven months pregnant and hoping to make it through finals before the baby arrived."

She hadn't. Lori had been born May 5.

"I did know you."

"No, Logan. You remembered us as kids. You didn't remember asking me to be your wife. You didn't remember loving me. And you didn't remember me telling you that Lori was your baby. I've tried many times since then, Logan. Your family finally asked me to stop, stop trying to make you remember when you couldn't."

And now came another difference. On previous occasions he emphatically denied this version of events. He often accused her of lying about telling him and then denying also that there was anything wrong with his memory. Not this time. This time he nodded his acceptance that she had tried and failed.

"I can remember now."

"But back then you could barely speak. The doctors didn't know if your condition was permanent. Up until last year, you were still slurring your words, struggling to find them and your short-term memory was—"

"So let me get this straight. You and Connor and my father all decided, together, that it would be best to stop telling me that I had a daughter?"

Chapter Nineteen

"I'm a father?" Logan asked. The pain of his family's betrayal cut through him like shards of broken glass even as the joy of knowing Lori was his bubbled up inside him.

"Yes."

"And my own family didn't want me to know?"

"It's more complicated than that."

"Maybe you should speak slower, so I can follow you." His pain had morphed into sarcasm and he thought he was entitled to it.

She had her hands over her eyes now and had folded at the waist as if the effort of remaining upright was beyond her. She looked like a marathon runner just after crossing the finish line.

When she spoke, her words were hoarse and trembling. "I keep waiting for you to remember me. I kept hoping. But you haven't. Then you tell me our lovemaking is as you imagined it. We've made love before in this very bed. And that day you told me you were saving for something, but you can't remember what. It was for us. For our wedding."

"Us?" He sounded simpler than he'd become, he thought. He managed to close his mouth before she straightened and dropped her hands limply to her lap.

But he knew. In his twisting stomach, he knew. She

had been waiting to see if he would get better. Everyone told him that he was not the same man who shipped out to Iraq. That was the man she had loved. Not the one who had come back. It was the reason he had not asked her out since his return.

In a strange way, it was as if she'd betrayed him. She might not have been unfaithful, but she'd given up trying when he needed love the most. She'd abandoned him and that meant that she wasn't who he thought she was.

"You should have told me every day."

Paige flapped her arms. "I did! And every day it hurt you and every day you forgot. I *am* telling you, now. Again. But I don't know if you'll remember this conversation."

He wanted to remember her, remember them. But the brain injury had stolen that piece of him. "I'll remember this conversation until I die."

She stared at him, eyes wide, as if looking at a stranger. She was weeping now, tears rolling down her cheeks, and inside him the storm raged and blew.

"You loved me. How could you forget that? It hurts me, Logan. You hurt me."

Her pain couldn't compare to his, though. She'd walked away when he needed her in his life, an anchor. What if they had married? Would she have pretended that hadn't happened because she couldn't face being with someone…defective?

He stood, needing to put distance between them. Not trusting himself not to lash out with the pain. She felt the injured party. He felt that, too, because she'd thought him incompetent. She'd been waiting for his brain to magically heal so he could access those parts of his brain damaged beyond repair. And she blamed him for going away and coming back like this.

Well, he blamed her for giving up on him. He might not be the man he had been when he went away. But he was still a man. And he was capable of being a father.

"I've lived next door to my daughter nearly all her life and neither of us knew."

"I kept hoping you'd come back."

"I am back." He practically shouted it.

Here he'd loved her all this time but thought that she'd never settle for a man with his issues. And that turned out to be true. She'd been waiting for the man he had been before the building had crashed down on them and he'd been hit with a chunk of concrete.

"Paige, I do love you and I love Lori. It cuts me to realize you didn't see that."

"I saw. But that's not always enough."

What did that mean? What else did she need from him?

"Was it that hard for you to stand by me? Would you have left me in the dark if we had married?"

She'd gone pale. "I don't know. Maybe I would have done that to protect Lori."

"Protect her from what? From me?" That was crazy. But his heart was hammering, just knowing that something had happened. Something that scared her enough to do this.

Paige summoned all her courage.

"You know that scar on Lori's chin and jaw?"

Then she held his gaze as she told him about Lori's fall and his failure to protect her. She watched as her words tore him apart.

"I'm sorry, Logan. I have to protect Lori."

From downstairs came the sound of people stomping the snow from their boots on the porch.

Logan turned toward the sound. "Is that a drum?"

A moment later the front door banged open, and Lori's voice echoed up the stairs.

"Mom! We're home and we have pizza!"

They stared at each other. His mistake only served to drive her point home like the point of a sword.

"Not a drum," he whispered.

Paige scrambled to tug on the rest of her clothing. When she turned, it was to find Logan staring at her. He was barefoot and dressed in his jeans and a snug black T-shirt.

"Where are you going?" he asked.

"To tell Lori."

Now he was shaking his head. "No. Don't."

"Logan, you can do this. They are all wrong. You'll remember this time. I know it. You can be a dad. You can."

"I might hurt her again. Make a mistake, think I hear birds when she's calling me."

"She's not an infant anymore."

He was still shaking his head. "I thought I could take care of Stephen and Valerie. I was just kidding myself."

"You can. Logan, you just saved my life and Lori's. Without you, we would have died in that fire."

"The state would be crazy to give me custody."

He sat on the bed, cradling his face in his hands.

"I'm going to tell her, Logan."

He reached out and grabbed her by the wrist, staying her. She knelt before him.

"Logan. It's time. She needs you. You need her."

"My father?"

"Is not making this decision. We are. Her parents."

"Her parents," he whispered, as if trying on the title.

Paige went to find her daughter. Mr. Lynch, Lori and

the Sullivan kids were in the family room sliding slices of pizza onto paper plates as Mr. Lynch scrolled through a list of possible movie choices. They agreed to wait to begin until Lori returned.

"Where is Grandma?" asked Paige.

"Kitchen, making a salad to go with pizza. I finished my homework at school before dance," said Lori, making the logical assumption as to the reason for the conversation.

Paige paused in the formal living room that sat between the family room and the dining room, where Logan now waited. He'd come down after her. She'd never seen him look so petrified.

"Do you remember asking me to speak to your dad and ask him if he wanted to be in your life?"

Lori stilled and her eyes went round. "Yes."

"Well, up until a few minutes ago, he didn't know he had a daughter. It was a shock for him."

"But he wants to see me?"

"Instantly. That's what he wanted. Truthfully, he's mad at me for keeping you a secret."

"Can we call him?" asked Lori.

Paige went down on one knee and rested a hand on her daughter's shoulder. "You don't need to call him. He's here. He's been here. Lori, honey, you already know him."

Her daughter's eyes went rounder still and her fine dark brows lifted. She looked like Logan when she did that. She had his brown hair and those stunning deep amber eyes, both just slightly lighter than Logan's.

Lori's gaze shifted toward the dining room and she stiffened. Paige knew instinctively that Logan was there. A turn of her head confirmed her suspicion. Logan was staring at Lori, seeing her again but for the first time.

"Hiya," he said.

Lori glanced to her mom and then back to Logan. "Him?"

Paige nodded. "Yes, him. Logan Lynch is your father, honey."

Lori stepped away from her then and walked with deliberate steps toward Logan, who was swallowing as if something was stuck in his throat.

"Should I call you dad?" she asked.

But Logan didn't answer. Instead, he scooped Lori up in his arms and pressed her small body to his chest as he wept. Lori clung to his neck and she began to cry, as well.

Paige's throat closed as she realized the magnitude of the mistake that she had made in waiting so long. The pain and joy of their meeting tore her to shreds. She'd had no right to deny them. Injury or no injury, Logan was Lori's father. Clearly, he loved her with all his heart.

Finally, Logan settled his gangly legged daughter on his hip as if she were still a toddler. Lori didn't let go of him, keeping her legs and arms locked around him.

"You can call me whatever you like," he said, answering the question she'd posed many minutes before. He glanced to her.

She mouthed the words, *I'm sorry.*

His chin lifted and his dark eyes went cold. "You should be."

She had been angry at him for reenlisting. But that had faded and she'd tried so hard to make him remember them. But it had been too soon. Now, perhaps, she was too late. Her timing, again, was bad. All she knew for certain was that Lori no longer needed protecting from Logan. What her daughter needed was her father.

"Can I tell people?" asked Lori.

"Yes," said Logan, wiping his wet cheeks with the back of one hand.

Lori wriggled, and Logan set her down. Lori took his hand. "Come on. Let's tell your dad."

Logan blinked but did not move as Lori tugged. She paused and stared up at him.

"He's a grandfather," said Logan. "He's *your* grandfather."

"That's right," said Lori, making the connection.

"I have a grandfather."

"I hope he's sitting down," said Logan. The pair walked past her as if she were invisible. She half hoped that she was. When she glanced toward the kitchen, it was to find her mother standing in the doorway holding a fresh green salad in the palm of one hand and forks in the other.

"What did you just do?"

Chapter Twenty

Her mother was mad at Paige for not consulting her before deciding to tell Logan once more about fathering her child. Logan's father was supportive, but Beverly was doing a fine imitation of an Amish shunning. At least Steven and Valerie lent their support, after Paige's mother had finished with that "I'm disappointed" lecture. Paige finally gave up and went to bed in the Lynches' home, since her bedroom was a charred ruin, and hoped that tomorrow someone in this house, besides Logan's father, would speak to her.

Sometimes she really hoped her mother would stop speaking to her.

The next morning the kids poured down the stairs the moment they heard the words *snow day*. She had a rare opportunity to use the bathroom alone and tried again to wash off the stubborn stink of the fire. When she reached the kitchen for breakfast, her greeting was met with silence. Paige's mother wasn't speaking to her. Logan wasn't speaking to her. Mr. Lynch was speaking to her but he kept giving her a sympathetic look followed by a slow shake of his head. The kids didn't seem to be shunning her, so much as being preoccupied with pancakes and planning their free day.

Overnight the world had turned white. Six inches of

fresh snow had already fallen with another four predicted. The schools and local businesses were closed, including Rathburn-Bramley. Lori, Steven and Valerie were already making plans to go sledding on the hill beside the cemetery. Long ago she and Logan and Connor had done the very same thing.

Steven tried unsuccessfully to get Logan to come along but he told the children that constables didn't get snow days. She offered to join them and her suggestion was met with underwhelming acceptance.

Her mother gave her the cold shoulder when she offered to take over making the pancakes, saying she could handle it. Paige retreated to the dining room with her paper plate, napkin and silverware.

Her daughter left her plate and charged up the stairs, returning a few minutes later carrying two of Valerie's sweatshirts and one of Steven's. Her own coat was over at their house, which was still closed for the fire inspector, so Paige helped her zip one of Valerie's that was so tight, she could barely lift her arms.

This morning Lori had been the only one among them who did not seem angry by her lie of omission. But one look at her daughter's face told her that the morning's smiles and giggles were only for her grandparents and father. Her daughter rummaged in a communal basket for mittens and a hat. Steven and Valerie, already in their winter attire, were in the back shed, retrieving their sleds and one flying saucer.

This left Paige momentarily alone with Lori.

"You should have told me," said her daughter.

Lori stood before her, pale and somber, with her borrowed ski hat askew.

"Sweetheart."

"You told me he left us. That he wasn't coming back.

But he's been here all along." Lori's voice trembled. Logan looked out at her from those familiar light brown eyes, accusing her of stealing from them both.

"Lori, honey. He *did* leave us. He reenlisted."

"Why didn't you tell me?"

"Because when you were little, I told Logan you were his daughter but he couldn't remember things very well back then. He kept forgetting me and you. Because of that, his doctors and his family didn't think he could be a good dad."

"He's not dumb, Mom. He's smart and funny and nice."

"Yes," said Paige. "He's all those things, but he doesn't remember us."

Lori thrust her hands, now in pink mittens, to her hips. "Then we tell him the stuff that he forgot."

LOGAN HAD NEARLY put his SUV in the ditch before he'd even left the driveway. So he'd parked his vehicle and walked the half mile to Connor's place because his brother had a snowmobile.

West Main Street was empty. It seemed folks were heeding the warnings to stay off the roads.

Because of the size of the county, Hornbeck did not see any of the state's snowplows until after the main highways were cleared. Generally, that was hours after they set out.

He walked past the Sullivan place and checked that the home seemed undisturbed. It stood silent and empty amid the unbroken blanket of snow. Next, he trudged past the funeral home. That also looked closed up tight. But he knew that there was at least one person there. Ursula Sullivan's body lay in the basement cooling lockers; the funeral was planned for next Saturday.

Logan knocked and paused to stomp the snow off his boots before letting himself in through Connor's back door. He found his brother on the phone in his kitchen, talking about schedules, deliveries and payments while wearing his woolen overcoat. Logan assumed the topic of conversation was the real estate business, which was funny. Who would want to see a house in this weather?

The real estate business slowed to a stop in the months between Thanksgiving and Christmas. Connor said people just stayed put for the holidays.

Logan left his coat on because it was so cold inside that he could see his breath.

Connor dropped the phone into his coat pocket. Then he lifted his brows and waited for Logan to speak.

It was so hard not to jump right to the accusation that Connor had drugged Paige. Logan strained against the need to find out if it were true. But he knew Connor and that he didn't always tell the truth.

His brother frowned as the silence stretched.

Logan did not want to believe that Connor could have done this. The need to warn him that he was under suspicion warred with the itch to punch him. Should he disregard the sheriff's request and try for an honest conversation?

"The heat off?" asked Logan.

Connor hesitated. "Yup. I'm waiting for the service guy. What's up?"

"Wasn't it off last time I was here?"

Connor shifted from side to side. "It's an old house."

That answered his question. If his brother would not even be honest about the heat, he wasn't going to fess up to drugging Paige.

He looked at Connor, seeing past his idol, and to

the man who shifted from side to side, his mouth tight and scowling.

He was planning to tell Connor about Lori, that he was an uncle, but then Logan remembered that Connor already knew. Had known from the start. It was another wall between them. Connor could have told him anytime instead of helping convince Lori that it was too soon to try again.

"You hear about the fire?"

"Yeah. I did. Heard you pulled Paige and her kid out before the firetrucks got there. That makes you a hero all over again. Do they know how it started?"

Logan's eyes narrowed. Did Connor know? Logan met his brother's watery eyes. Finally, Connor glanced away.

"Never mind," said Connor. "I'll ask the guys at the fire department. Geesh. You want coffee?"

Logan shook his head. "I need to borrow your snowmobile."

"My snowmobile?" His gaze swept over Logan, resting on the snow that caked his pant legs from the knee down. "Did you walk here in this storm?"

"Too dangerous to drive."

Connor shook his head in disapproval. Then he got the keys to the snowmobile and tossed them. Logan caught them in the air.

"You're getting better," said Connor, giving him a half smile.

In addition to a beautiful home and luxury SUV, Connor owned a motorcycle and boat that he was forever trying to get Paige and Lori to join him on. He also had the snowmobile that Logan often borrowed to race around on the logging trails and pathways threading through the surrounding woods. Lately, he used it to look in on folks in town who were housebound or needed checking on. Once, when the river had frozen, they had even taken it all the way to the town of Ouleout for breakfast. Logan envied his big brother sometimes. A big success in local politics and in real estate. Seemed everything he touched turned to gold.

Logan never questioned Connor's success, until this minute. Was he a business whiz or did the cash come from elsewhere?

"Something else?" asked Connor.

Logan told him that he knew about his daughter, Lori, and that he hoped that he and Paige might work things out between them. When he finished, Connor was sitting at his kitchen table with one elbow on the surface and his hand clutching his forehead. He looked sick. Logan wondered if it was not his stomach, but his brother's conscience that was bothering him.

"You all right?" asked Logan.

"It's a lot. You and Paige and a kid."

"Paige tells me that you knew from the start," said Logan.

That news brought his other hand up to form a tent over his eyes. Logan waited for Connor to look up. It took a while. His brother seemed upset, and Logan couldn't tell if Connor was mad at Paige for ignoring the wishes of his family telling him about Lori or sad because Connor's chances with Paige had completely tanked. He still thought his brother had feelings for Paige.

"What are you going to do?" asked Connor.

"About what?"

"Well, are you getting a lawyer? Visitation rights and that sort of thing?"

Logan hadn't even thought of that.

"We're all living in the same house."

"Are you listed as the parent on Lori's birth certificate?"

"I don't know."

"You need a lawyer. Call Joe Dickson."

Logan nodded, but didn't say more. He still didn't know if he could trust his brother.

Connor offered coffee again but Logan had already stayed too long and headed back out to his office on the snowmobile.

When he got in, it was to his office phone ringing incessantly.

"Hello, Constable Lynch speaking."

"Finally. It's Detective Albritton of the state police. I want to follow up with you on a few things. First, the charges against Dr. Morris on possession of a controlled substance. We found no evidence that Dr. Morris ever touched the bag containing the oxycodone or any of the bottles containing the drugs."

"So how did she get them into the bag?"

"Gloves. Whoever brought them in wore gloves. What we need to figure out is who that someone might be."

"What about the check?"

"The deposit in Dr. Morris's account was electronic. Made from an account in the Grand Caymans. Untraceable, as far as we can determine."

"So you can't tell who sent it or why."

"But they had her checking account number and bank routing number. Someone had to give that to them."

Logan's speech was slow as he answered because when he hurried, he stammered. "Her employer would have that information or someone working there. Maybe it was the same person who planted those drugs in her home."

"It's a theory. I understand from Sheriff Trace that Paige believes your older brother, Connor Lynch, might have given her the drugs found in her system."

"That is what she told me and what I told him."

"And that he had time and opportunity to plant that bag of drugs when he brought her home."

"But I don't know how he would have obtained them."

"Well, I'm sorry and I hope she is wrong."

"Me, too."

"Also I heard that there was a house fire yesterday."

"Yes. The second floor of the Morrises' residence is gone, along with the roof."

"Along with any evidence, like a missing check book," said Albritton. "Ask Dr. Morris to phone me. She's not answering her mobile."

"Lost in the fire," said Logan.

"Oh, I see. Where is she staying?"

"With me. At my father's place."

"All right. Can I have your mobile, then, Constable?"

Logan gave it to him.

"Sheriff Trace will be down to speak to Paige sometime today. He's on his way there to see you but the snow is causing havoc on the highways. We've got multiple accidents and stranded drivers so I'm not certain when he'll be there."

"I'll be on the lookout for him."

PAIGE HAD ANOTHER serious conversation with both her mother and with Mr. Lynch while the kids were sledding in the yard. She'd been relieved when she could finally slip into a borrowed coat and head out to the hill beside the cemetery. She'd even taken a few runs with the kids before they waded back through the heavy snow toward home for lunch. The plows had been through, but they just couldn't keep up with the accumulations. There were two inches of fresh powder on the road since the plow's run. In the unplowed spots, their steps crunched through the layer of ice between yesterday's snow, the freezing rain and the newest coating.

On West Main, they turned toward the Lynches' home. She could not keep from glancing at the ruined house next door. The upper floors were blackened and icicles continued to grow from the water left by the fire department.

"You kids go inside," she said.

They piled past her, stomping off some of the snow that clung to their boots before they reached the door and then slipped inside.

It wasn't until she reached the Lynches' porch that she spotted the twin tire tracks and then the red truck parked before her mother's garage. She knew the vehicle. The fire inspector was back.

"Ms. Morris?" called Inspector Frick as he emerged from his truck. "Just coming to see you."

And the day just got better and better, she thought. She raised a hand in greeting, her wet gloves and sodden cuffs contacting her exposed wrist, making her shiver. She waited for him to cross through the yard to where she stood on the porch.

He hesitated and then climbed the stairs.

"A few more questions," he said, taking out his recorder and holding it and his open pad before him. He removed his glove to flick on the recorder. The red light glowed bright as a stoplight between them. With a flick of his thumb, he readied his pen.

"You said you had three smoke detectors?"

"Yes."

"Locations?"

"In the kitchen, the top of the bedroom stairs and in the hallway outside our bedrooms."

"Only they are all in the kitchen."

She cocked her head. She must have heard that wrong.

"What's that now?"

"All three were in the kitchen, on the chopping block, disabled." He pointed his pen in the direction of the fire-scorched building.

"That's impossible."

"I have photos," he said. "Would you know why all three smoke detectors were in the kitchen with the batteries removed?" Frick asked.

"I don't know."

Frick jotted a note on the pad.

Paige's heart was now hammering like a woodpecker after a dead tree. There were spots before her eyes. She'd lost her job, her home and been accused of drug possession and now this man was about to pin this fire on her. What should she do?

"You find out who did this," she said to herself.

"What's that, Ms. Morris?"

"It is Dr. Morris. And I am telling you to find out who did this. If this fire was set, if someone tampered with our smoke detectors, then it's more than arson."

"Sometimes when people are distraught…"

"I'm not distraught."

He continued as if she had not spoken. "Accused of drug abuse, fired from their job."

"I am suspended pending a hearing."

"They feel hopeless."

"Are you suggesting that I disabled my own smoke detectors and then set my mother's house on fire with my entire family inside?"

"It's possible."

"My daughter?"

"Possible, again."

"Why would I do that?"

"To end your life and the pain."

"Where is your evidence that I did this? Do you have a suicide note?"

"Many suicide victims do not leave notes."

"Are my fingerprints on the detectors?" Even as she said this, she knew the answer. Of course they were. She changed the batteries every spring on daylight savings.

"Yes, and only yours."

"Ask me if I set that fire," she said, ready to fight now.

Frick sucked in a breath through flaring nostrils and then faced Paige. "Did you set the fire that burned your mother's home and nearly killed both you and your daughter?"

"No," she said.

"I can come back with the police."

"I expect you will. But the next time you set up an interrogation, I'll have my attorney present."

The inspector stepped off the porch. Paige felt the tension between her shoulders begin to ease. There he paused to glance back at her. The digital recorder's light still glowed red.

"Do you know anyone who might want to cause your family harm?" asked Frick.

"Perhaps whoever killed Edward Sullivan and drugged his wife might also have set this fire." And drugged her, as well. Connor. She didn't want to think him capable of such acts, but she couldn't stop herself from considering the possibility. Had Connor drugged her because he had been trying to make a move on her, or was he tied up in whatever was happening at Rathburn-Bramley?

"Do you have any evidence to that effect?"

She shook her head. All she had was a churning stomach and the feeling that she was free-falling out of an airplane.

Frick shut off the recorder.

"I'm just pursuing my investigation. My early estimation is that someone set this fire. If not you, I need to ask who that someone might be."

"I don't know."

Frick headed down the steps of the Lynch home. There in the fast-falling snow, he turned. "We found kerosene in the garage. It is likely the same type of propellant used on the main staircase in your home. Only your fingerprints, again."

"Would a suicidal woman place the detectors in the kitchen, remove the batteries and then return the kerosene to the garage before setting the fire?"

"Still an investigation."

"Did you find a lighter upstairs?"

"Can't comment."

"Well, I know I didn't do it, which means that someone was inside my home. Disabled the smoke detectors. Threw kerosene on the stairs and then lit a match."

"Seems so," said Frick.

"That's not just arson," said Paige. "It's attempted murder. Someone is setting me up."

Frick regarded her for a long, silent moment.

"If what you say is true, then you appear to have some very powerful and determined enemies. You should be asking yourself who would benefit from your disappearance?"

Chapter Twenty-One

It was half past three in the afternoon when Logan's mobile rang. He checked the caller ID. It was Paige. He did not want to speak to her, needed a little time to understand and accept her decision to shut him out. He let the call go to voicemail.

Was this all his fault?

He'd reenlisted against the wishes of his fiancée, without even consulting her, and he'd been so hurt she'd asked him to postpone the wedding. She said that this had upset him enough to break their engagement. This man he had been was like a stranger to him. He'd do anything to have Paige, including postponing their wedding.

But according to her, her dad had just died. Her mother was in terrible debt and she had to assume debt herself to finish school. Had swooping in like a hero been such a terrible thing for him to do?

Perhaps. Marriage was a partnership. He could understand Paige's anger when he took serious steps without consulting her, reenlisting to help her without asking if that was the help she wanted. But he still struggled with her withholding the information about their relationship and his daughter for so long without trying again. When had his short-term memory improved?

He just didn't know because he didn't remember it

being impaired in the first place. He thought of Lori's scarred jaw and a shiver danced across his back. Paige had been protecting Lori from a father who was impaired. If their roles had been reversed, what would he have done?

A large SUV with chains on the tires pulled up to his office. The vehicle was salt and mud-spattered, black and bore no markings. He watched out the window as Sheriff Axel Trace climbed from the passenger seat and adjusted his hat low over his eyes to keep the snow from reaching his face. Trace was tall and broad and wearing his official sheriff's jacket with the patch of Onutake County.

Logan glanced toward the driver, wondering who that might be. When the driver rounded the hood, he noted it was a woman who was not much taller than the grill. Logan blinked at the diminutive figure. She wore sunglasses and a puffy gray coat that reached her knees. The boots on her feet were practical and salt-stained. She had fine, chin-length blond hair capped with a navy blue ski hat. The bold yellow letters on the hat said DHS.

By the time they reached his door, snow had stuck to her cap and accumulated on the brim of his hat.

He shook hands with Trace and waited for introductions.

"Constable Lynch, this is Homeland Security Agent Rylee Hockings. She heard from Detective Albritton about the recent death of a member of the Rathburn-Bramley product assurance team and the trafficking arrest and wanted to speak to Dr. Morris. We also understand, again from Albritton, that Dr. Morris is under suspension from her workplace and under at least two investigations."

"Two?"

"Trafficking and arson."

"Ah, I hadn't heard about the arson."

"And there was a large sum of money recently deposited in her bank account," said Hockings. "I'm very interested in speaking to Dr. Morris. Would you know what products they make down at that plant? Their website is vague."

"Opiates. Gases for anesthesiologists."

"Vaccines?" asked Hockings. "Flu vaccines?"

"I don't know," said Logan. "Why?"

"Ongoing investigation," said Hockings.

Logan nodded. Her investigation seemed a one-way street with her collecting information but offering none.

"Well, last I saw Paige, she was over at my father's house. She and her family are staying with us because of the fire. Would you like me to ride out with you?" asked Logan.

Hockings looked at the snowmobile parked before her gigantic SUV and checked the time on her phone.

The two exchanged a look of concern.

"I need to speak to Connor Lynch regarding the information Constable Lynch shared with me," said Trace.

"We need to pick up Drake first," said Hockings.

Logan knew of only one person named Drake. That would be Allen Drake, the CEO of Rathburn-Bramley.

"He could save us a trip," said Trace.

They returned their attention to him.

Hockings nodded then turned to Logan. "Will you go and get Dr. Morris and bring her to the plant? I would like her there when we go to the production floor."

"Now?" he asked. The afternoon gloom and snow made it seem to be already growing dark, though it was not yet four in the afternoon.

"Yes. We'll pick up Drake and meet you at the plant."

"The plant is closed today for the snow emergency," said Logan.

"I've contacted Drake. He's the CEO. He'll give us access to the production areas." Hockings aimed a gloved finger at Logan. "Get Dr. Morris and meet us at the plant. If you beat us there, just sit tight."

"Yes, ma'am."

PAIGE HAD HER own boots on and her feet in dry socks. That was something, anyway.

Spending much of the morning with the kids had shown her that not everything in the world was bleak. But the fire inspector's visit had dampened her mood and the news that he had cleared the scene did not cheer her.

Her mother had been to their church this morning and returned with a bounty of donated clothing for them all. That made Paige hopeful again and together, dressed in hand-me-down items, she and her mother headed over to their house.

They spent the afternoon sorting through the frozen, water-logged mess of downstairs and the charred ruin of the second floor.

The house was freezing inside, but fortunately, their coats were stored in the coat closet downstairs and had avoided getting soaked by the water sprayed by the fire department on the upper floors. The garments did, however, smell like a fire pit.

It was terrifying to see the walls, where she and Lori, had slept, blackened and burned to the studs. There was nothing salvageable from the upper level. Thankfully, the closed bookshelves and the chest of drawers downstairs had protected the photo albums. Many of the framed photos were ruined but she had more than a few of them safely stored on the cloud.

They would have to begin again. Clothing and personal care items were Paige's priority. She would take her mom and Lori shopping just as soon as the insurance money arrived.

"Have you called the insurance company yet?" she asked her mother.

Her mom stopped and dropped the armful of photo albums on the dining room table.

"Not yet."

"You have to file a claim. You have to do that right away."

Her mother turned and leaned back against the table, gripping the edge with blackened fingers.

"I let the policy lapse."

"What? No!"

"Paige, I can't manage it all. It's too much."

"But, Mom. I moved in with you to help you. I pay you every month. It's enough to cover the expenses including insurance."

"Well, it isn't. I thought I'd save a few dollars. I mean, you have the smoke detectors and the CO detectors and the volunteer department is right down the road. I never thought…"

"I can't believe you didn't tell me. Consult me."

Her mother huffed. "You're a fine one to be talking about consulting people."

Paige turned her back as anger and guilt collided inside her like two rivers.

"Connor was by while you were sledding. He said he has lots of room. He said he'd be happy to have us all stay there at his place."

"No."

"But why? He's got a good job and a big house. And

you love that house. What is wrong with taking him up
on his offer?"

"Because his offer comes with strings," said Paige.
She'd already turned down his marriage proposal, twice.
Leave it to Connor to smell desperation and be there to
"help." And she still had her suspicions about him drugging her at the Harvest Festival.

"Well, Albert said we could stay with them as long
as we like."

"I will rent us an apartment."

"Hmm," said her mother. "With what?"

"I make a good salary and…" Her words trailed off.
She was suspended and her prospects at Rathburn-
Bramley looked dim. "I'll get a new job."

"Where? In Washington, DC, again?"

"Virginia."

Her mother waved a hand. "This community has been
my home for nearly forty years. My church, my book club
and my golf and bowling leagues are here. My friends
are here. I'm not leaving."

The thought of leaving Logan and Albert behind with
the two Sullivan kids hurt her, and Paige paused, thinking. When had Steven and Valerie become among the
people she counted as family?

She pictured them, her and Logan, with three children
and perhaps more. But first she'd have to get him to speak
to her. He was justifiably angry at her. She'd made decisions based on what she knew at the time. But as he had
improved, she had held on to her grievances and her old
fears. Now she feared she might lose him.

"What are you thinking about?" asked her mother,
her voice cautious.

"Marrying Logan."

"What? Don't be silly."

"It's not silly. I could marry him and we could adopt Steven and Valerie."

"I think your daughter might have something to say about that."

"I'll check with her."

"But not with me?"

"We are having a conversation right now, Mom."

"Well, I don't approve."

"I'll take you off the guest list."

"Don't be smart with me. He's got permanent brain damage. He's different, Paige. Admit it."

Logan was different because he was better. This man would never leave her to fend for herself as his younger self had done. This man would stay and protect her until the bitter end. Now she hoped that end was still far, far away.

He had a heart as big as the outdoors and a protective instinct a mile wide and paternal instincts as strong as steel. For the second time in her life, she wanted to marry Logan.

Logan's father's words came to her.

Instead of mourning the man he was, celebrate the man he is.

Outside, a motor rumbled.

"Who's that?" asked her mother, peering out the soot-stained window at the snowmobile that roared into the Lynches' front yard. "Oh, it's prince charming on his steed."

"Sarcasm doesn't become you, Mother."

"Connor is the smart choice."

She headed toward the door. "I'll send Lori and the kids over to help you carry things."

"Abandoning me," said her mother, using a shooing motion with both sooty hands. "Go ahead."

Paige made it across the yard as Logan turned off the snowmobile and headed toward his house. He spotted her and changed direction.

"Logan, I need to talk to you about what happened. What is happening."

"I agree. But I need to take you to the plant first."

"The plant? It's closed."

He told her about the visit from the sheriff and the Homeland Security agent and all the rest as her mother moved to the porch to eavesdrop.

"They need you on the production floor to help them figure out what might be happening inside."

Fresh, sweet, cold air filled her lungs. She straightened, coming back to life. The possibility of finding out what was happening, perhaps discovering who was attacking her and her family, invigorated her. Finally, she had a chance to fight back.

"Yes. Let's go."

Chapter Twenty-Two

In other circumstances, the ride to the plant might have been fun, exciting even. Paige sat behind Logan as they buzzed over West Main Street, taking the back route over the Raquette River and through Township Valley to Pearl. The snow was deep and unbroken except for driveways cleared by industrious residents in anticipation of the plow's arrival.

From Pearl Street, Logan veered off the road because they were free to cut across the fields and approach the factory from the opposite side. Paige clung tight and thrilled to the speed and the cold wind rushing past them, burning her cheeks until they tingled.

She wanted to tell Logan she was sorry and that she needed him in her life. She craved the chance to begin again. But for this moment, it was enough to hold him and shout with joy to the darkening sky as Logan made a sharp turn, sending fresh powder out behind them like a breaking wave. His laughter spilled back to her and she hugged him tighter, resting her cheek on his shoulder. He released one side of the handlebar grips to cradle her head in his hand for just a moment.

The beam of their single headlight bounced over the field before them as they flew onto Elm. Here he slowed and her mood changed. The side of the production plant loomed before them, rising from the field of white like a great gray ocean liner.

They had arrived and she'd be meeting with Homeland Security agents and sheriffs and her CEO. She'd only ever spoken to Allen Drake once during her employment interviews. Somehow, she'd become the hound, sent in to sniff out trouble. What was she doing? She didn't even know if she could find the product batch they were looking for. If she'd been the one trying to hide it, that production series would have been down the drain and all evidence destroyed. They'd had days to do just that. Did the sheriff think the evidence would be sitting out in a pretty package for them to unwrap?

Logan slowed and switched off the light.

"What's wrong?" she asked.

He lifted his gloved hand and pointed.

There, across the parking lot, a single box truck sat at the loading bay. One dock door was up and light spilled out around the truck. Beyond the vehicle were two sets of tire tracks marking the path the driver had taken across the lot from Raquette Road.

"That's not right," she said. "Who is that?"

Logan switched off the snowmobile. They were sitting in Centennial Park at the tree line that bordered the Rathburn-Bramley parking area. She'd walked here at lunch on beautiful sunny days to sit on a park bench or picnic table with coworkers. But tonight the trees swayed with the wind from the nor'easter that seemed to be just gearing up. The heavily falling snow and the darkness obscured her vision. But she could see two men outside the truck. They were holding something.

"Are those rifles?" she asked.

Logan reached inside his coat and pulled out a pair of compact binoculars.

"They are," he said.

"What are they doing in a snowstorm with rifles?"

"Nothing good." Logan turned his head, sweeping the area, suddenly the marine once more. "I don't see the vehicle from Homeland Security. It's a big black SUV."

"They should have beaten us here. Shouldn't they?"

Logan lowered the binoculars. "Probably. They were picking up your CEO."

"What do we do?"

"Call them." Logan pulled his phone from his side pocket, but the call failed. The next three attempts yielded the same result.

"Try a text."

He did but received the *not delivered* message.

"The storm?" she asked.

"Probably."

"What now?"

"Well, I'm not approaching armed men. The village didn't want me armed. Afraid I'd have a flashback, probably."

"Seems a bad decision in hindsight." She leaned out to watch the guards, backlit by the bright fluorescents inside the loading dock. "So we wait?"

He nodded.

"What if that's the shipment?"

"It likely is. Why else would they be moving it when the plant was closed and in this storm?"

"And we should just let it go?"

"Paige, I'm not riding you into danger. Homeland Security has resources. They can find and stop that truck."

As if on cue, into the lot slid a large black SUV. The guards took cover on the opposite side of the box truck.

"They don't see them," said Paige.

Logan turned on the snowmobile and flashed the light.

The guards turned toward them.

Both doors opened on the SUV and two people emerged. Behind the truck, the guards dropped to the snow-covered ground and lifted their rifles.

"Look out!" Paige yelled.

"Take cover!" shouted Logan.

The guards opened fire. The figure on the passenger side of the vehicle dropped. The second returned fire with a handgun.

"Outgunned," said Logan.

"Look," said Paige and pointed toward the loading dock. Two more gunmen appeared and opened fire, peppering the SUV with bullet holes. The single gunman scrambled behind the vehicle and to their downed partner. Paige watched in horror as the driver managed to get the wounded passenger back in the vehicle and get the SUV moving in reverse.

"They're leaving us."

He flicked off the light and moved them along the tree line and out of the scope of fire. Paige could see the flash of the muzzles as the gunmen fired at them, but the sound did not penetrate the roar of the motor.

She heard a whine behind them as they flashed up Elm and turned to see the bouncing light that could be only one thing—another snowmobile. Behind that came a second.

"They're after us," she shouted.

Logan glanced at the mirror fixed to the handlebars and then leaned forward.

"Hold on!"

Paige clung to Logan as they flashed through the park on the snowmobile. She wondered which of the two in the SUV had been shot and how badly they were injured.

Out of the park now, they flew over the snow up Turkey Hollow Road, and their pursuers were gaining on them. Something hit the back of the sled and the rear taillight winked out.

Gunfire. They were shooting at them. Paige imagined getting a bullet in her back. Leaving Lori and Steven and Valerie alone again. She had to survive this. They had to get away.

"Hold on!" Logan cut to the right between the church and the firehouse. The volunteer organization was the only building that looked open. Why didn't he go there?

They rode dangerously close to the steep hill that lay between the Methodist church below them and the firehouse above. She felt the pull and slide as he managed to hug the top of the slope.

"Get to a landline phone and call for help, Paige. Stay put. Don't go back there."

"What are you—"

Without explanation, he reached back and shoved her from the seat behind him.

Chapter Twenty-Three

Paige flew through space, arms out and screaming. She landed in deep snow and rolled. A moment later the snowmobiles chasing them flashed past her in hot pursuit of Logan. The vehicles darted up Railroad Avenue. Now it was Logan's back wide-open to gunfire.

Paige pushed herself to her feet, located her hat and struggled up the steep, slippery incline to the fire station.

There she found her daughter's third-grade teacher, Mr. Garrett, on duty in his volunteer firefighter shirt. He was holding a stained wooden spoon covered in red sauce when he buzzed her in.

"Ms. Morris. What a surprise. Just in time for dinner. I'm making chicken parm." His smile faded as he gave her a long look. "What's wrong?"

She told him as much as she could between the gasping and panting. She hurried to the phone and dialed 911. She got the county dispatch and explained the situation including the DHS vehicle and the shooting. By the time she put down the phone, the three men and one woman from the volunteer squad were suited up. There, in full firefighter gear, stood teachers Mr. Garrett and Mr. Warren, Mr. Booker, who was the husband of the school nurse and the head of human resources at the plant, and the school principal, Mrs. Unger.

"You can't go down there. They have guns."

Mrs. Unger, who had always inspired terror in Paige as a child, gave her a confident smile.

"So do we, Ms. Morris." She lifted the edge of her polar fleece jacket to reveal a shoulder holster.

Paige blurted out the first thing that came to her mind. "Do you carry that in school?"

"Of course not. But we aren't in school."

"Why do you think these men were not just armed security guards?"

"Automatic weapons. Body armor. They set up an ambush for the DHS agents and then they attacked us without provocation."

Unger nodded. "Then we had better stop that truck. You coming?"

She was. In only a few moments she and five members of the volunteer fire department of the village of Hornbeck were underway in their single hook and ladder truck. Behind them came their EMS vehicle, driven by Mr. Garrett.

As they headed back down Turkey Hollow Road, Mrs. Unger turned to Paige.

"Busy week for you."

LOGAN GLANCED BACK to see Paige land in deep snow and roll. A moment later his pursuers flashed past her position, following him. Logan had one advantage. He knew the territory. But his snowmobile was slower, and his pursuers had firearms. Logan was vulnerable and exposed.

Logan reached Creamery Road. Here he turned off the headlight. He knew this trail down the cutoff. He knew where the boulders had been pushed out of the way for the rough jeep trail and where the narrow bridge broached the fast-running stream. His pursuers did not.

He aimed for the creek and only veered toward the bridge at the last moment. As a result he slid sideways. The back part of the track left the bridge. He shifted forward, leaning out over the skis and the weight of his body and the engine was enough to keep him on the wooden trestles.

Behind him, his pursuers, on larger machines, did not make the turn so quickly. The first sled swerved and skidded across the start of the trestle and then fell off the side of the bridge. The snowmobile tipped and rolled, landing on the driver in the icy creek. The second driver started the turn and then abandoned the attempt so that he and his snowmobile careened down the incline, also landing in the stream.

Logan did not stop. He had to find Paige and be sure she was all right. He made it down the cutoff and over Turax Hollow Road, coming out between the school and Rathburn-Bramley. There he saw the red flashing lights of the village's fire truck, which had collided with the box truck he'd seen parked at the loading bay. The two vehicles blocked Raquette Road and the box truck had slipped off the shoulder. Logan's best guess, it wasn't getting out of that ditch without a tow truck.

He slowed at the accident and found Mr. Garrett standing at the back of the EMS vehicle.

"Where's Paige?" Logan asked.

"She went with Drake, the DHS agent and the sheriff."

"Where?"

"Into the plant."

"Is it clear?" asked Logan.

"I don't know, Logan. I only know that we are supposed to treat this truck as a biohazard and stay here with it until backup arrives."

"The driver?"

"Ran off." Garrett motioned in the direction of the woods.

Logan put the snowmobile in motion toward the glowing mouth of the open loading dock door, twisting the throttle for greater speed. She was in trouble. He just knew it.

PAIGE FOLLOWED BEHIND Sheriff Trace, now bleeding from his left shoulder. They reached the front entrance of the pharmaceutical plant. Drake had opened the door using the key code, and the sheriff had braced it with a cylindrical waste can to allow their eventual backup easy access. Before him was the CEO, looking pale and shaken after his arrival and clutching his key card as if it had some magical powers to grant invisibility. Leading the group was DHS Agent Rylee Hockings.

Paige had suggested waiting, but when Hockings had told her what they were facing and that this terrorist group was fully capable of releasing this pandemic in her hometown, Paige changed her mind. Her daughter lived here, the Sullivan kids and her mother and Logan's family. Everyone who was dear to her lived right here.

Hockings and the sheriff had been delayed in their arrival because they had slid off the road and it had taken some work by the three of them to get them back underway. They had arrived to take fire from the loading dock and reversed course. They had been on the front side of the building, out of sight of the loading dock, when the fire truck and EMS had arrived, forcing the box truck off the road.

Since Paige was the only one who knew the batch numbers from Dr. Sullivan's files and what sort of packaging and shipping containers to search for, she was included in the party heading to the factory.

Paige had joined Rathburn-Bramley's CEO in the backseat as they made a second approach. They had already tried and failed to make contact with Hocking by phone, but they did not have a signal. When Paige explained that she'd called the state police and told them the situation, Hockings and Sheriff Trace decided to go in via a different route.

Now knowing that their targets were on the loading dock and armed, they approached from the opposite direction, through the main entrance.

Hornbeck's volunteers remained back with the fire engine and EMS vehicle waiting for the DHS agents and state police.

Where was Logan? Had he evaded pursuit or was he out there in the snow, injured or dead? She pushed down the panic at that thought. If ever in her life she needed to focus, it was now.

They crept down the hall past the empty security station and through the silent metal detectors.

Hockings had said this group called themselves Siming's Army after some Chinese mythological creature that judged each person's worth to determine the number of days they had on earth. This group had successfully created a deadly, virulent strain of influenza that would rival the pandemic of 1918. She'd studied that epidemic in school. She knew that more people died in the two-year contagion than all the victims of WWI. Like a war, that illness did not take the young, old and weak. It killed people in their twenties and thirties at a rate of twelve percent. Paige had asked the mortality rate of this strain. The CDC had told Hockings that it would approach sixty percent.

Worse still, this contagion, once airborne, would not die on surfaces. It would spread with the speed of a gas leak, only undiluted, from host to host.

They paused in the data center at the bank of windows overlooking the finished goods area. Beyond was their destination: shipping.

"How do you know it's here?" she asked Hockings.

"Because we intercepted one shipment of both the vaccine and the pathogen. And because this is a perfect site for manufacturing this virus."

"And because they were shooting at us," added the sheriff.

"It could be in the box truck," said Paige.

"They wouldn't send the truck without armed guards. The driver fled. We watched him. The guards are here, so the product is here," said Hockings. "Our intelligence indicates that once production is complete the pathogen will be released in this state in locations where it will cause the highest mortality."

"But why?" asked Paige. "Why would anyone do this?"

"Not anyone. North Korea. A country we have choked with sanctions for years. Our people believe that they aimed to blame this attack on China, and for a time there, we believed that the Chinese were behind this. A rift between us and the Chinese would certainly benefit the North Koreans." Hockings looked down at the dark manufacturing floor. Only emergency lights glowed.

"What am I looking at, Drake?"

"That's where we manufacture pharmaceuticals. The upper level is management and quality control. Down here we have packaging, through those windows." He pointed straight ahead, at the darkness beyond. Then he pointed left, to another bank of dark observation windows. "That's finished goods and storage. The actual creation, brewing, we call it, and the filling floors are past packaging. Shipping adjoins filling, and the loading docks flank the building beyond that wall."

"Quickest route?"

Drake looked to Paige. "Through packaging, filling and shipping to the dock."

"Whatever they were shipping is still in here. We need to find it."

Hockings was confident that help would be coming, but Paige knew that there would be no air support. Helicopters would not fly in this. And the roads were now nearly impassable.

They entered the packaging floor, their footsteps echoing in the chamber filled with still conveyers, their metal rollers silent.

"What kind of doors between filling and shipping?" Sheriff Trace asked Drake.

"Uh…" Their CEO looked to her and she realized she'd never seen him on the filling floor.

"Fire doors," she said.

"Windows?"

"Yes," she said. "Safety glass. The kind with wires inside."

They crept along the wall and to the doors. Trace took one side and Hockings the other. Paige watched them gesture and nod in some language of which she was unfamiliar. Then the sheriff eased open his door. Light spilled across the concrete. Cold air crept along the floor, chilling her in her wet clothing.

Trace disappeared. Hockings whispered to them.

"Stay put."

Then Hockings disappeared after Trace. Drake looked at her with eyes wide and lips pressed into a grim line.

"Maybe we should move away from the doors," he said.

Paige shook her head. She was looking for the sort of shipping containers they would use to ensure an active virus was safe from breakage and protected from extreme temperatures.

The flu virus could survive up to two days outside the body on hard surfaces. But she knew how to kill it. Bleach. If this thing was a virus, bleach would kill it.

Paige cracked the door open and watched Hockings and Trace creep through the filling area and straight to shipping. Beyond lay the loading dock. After another series of unreadable gestures, they headed through the second set of doors.

Paige crept through the door after them to the shipping area where stacks of finished product lay in cardboard boxes awaiting transport to the loading docks.

"Stay here, she said," Drake whispered.

Paige left him behind, crossing to the doors leading to the loading dock. All those terrorists would need to do was toss one vial on the floor and they'd all be infected. They could be infected if one broke accidentally from, say…a bullet.

The shout came from the loading dock, Hocking's voice.

"DHS! Hands where we can see them."

The reply came in the form of automatic weapon fire.

Paige crouched beside the door, pressed up close to the small stack of boxes.

There was more shouting, and more shots fired. She knew one of the voices.

"That's Lou Reber, my head of security."

Paige jumped at the voice that came from beside her. Drake had made the move and followed her.

Next came two female voices ordering Lou to get the packages and get clear.

"That's Veronica," said Drake, his jaw now hanging open.

Veronica Vitale, the new CFO of Rathbun-Bramley. Paige recalled the day she was suspended. She'd been trooped out past Veronica Vitale and Lou Reber. The very two she had chosen not to contact with her discovery based on the assumption that her then boss, Dr. Ed Sullivan, would have reported the uninspected batch of product to one or both.

Another woman shouted to get the boxes.

"That's Carol Newman," Paige whispered.

"Who?" asked Drake.

"Sullivan's replacement."

"I didn't replace Sullivan."

Paige was certain the shock showed on her face.

Someone did, she thought.

Paige turned to Allen Drake to say as much when she noticed the boxes behind which they cowered. More important, she read the packing number on the sticker beside the mailing labels.

She'd looked at the hard copy of Dr. Sullivan's files often enough to recall the distinct series of numbers and letters. Now they made sense.

S6Y6M6INGAR666

Siming's Army and 666 and so on to 767. Twelve boxes and they were all right here.

"Sinclair, get to the serum," shouted Vitale.

"Sinclair?" asked Drake. "Park. He's my..."

"Head of productions," she finished for him.

Sinclair burst through the doors and turned toward them, coming up short at seeing them both squatting beside the boxes.

Drake roared and charged him. Sinclair lifted his pistol and fired twice. Drake grabbed his middle and crumpled to the cold floor. It gave Paige the moments she needed to run. She charged back out through the swinging doors. A shot broke the window above her head.

She darted between the stacked cardboard boxes as she ran a serpentine route back the way she had come.

"Morris! Come out and I won't kill you," shouted Sinclair.

Yeah, right, she thought, continuing toward the exit.

She made it through shipping to the filling area where three rows of production lines rested. Here they could package anything from a syringe of insulin to capsules of painkillers. Her heart hammered and her hands shook. She needed to go back and get those boxes. Every nerve in her body urged her to flee, to run home and hide under her bed as if she were six. But her mind raced with what she had to do. She must get all twelve of those boxes and destroy them. Which meant she had to keep from getting captured or killed.

Run. Then circle back.

She almost made it, too.

Chapter Twenty-Four

Logan drove the snowmobile to the main entrance of Rathburn-Bramley, slowing at sighting the familiar black SUV. The sheriff and DHS agent were likely inside. He parked behind a row of shrubbery and headed through the main entrance past the waste can someone had used to block open the door.

He'd been in this plant, but only as far as the metal detectors and once to Lou Reber's office on the rare occasion he needed to speak to the head of the company's security. Lou treated him as many here did, like a three-legged hunting dog. Not to be completely ignored, but useless, just the same.

His sense of direction was still good, so he headed toward the loading dock, passing through a room of boxed product bound together with clear plastic wrap. Next came the packaging area where the finished goods were obviously moved on conveyers into the flattened piles of cardboard boxes. He continued along the curving conveyor belts illuminated only by the red emergency lights above and on the exit doors. He paused at the next set of doors and peered through the glass. The emergency lighting gleamed off the shiny stainless-steel machinery. Perhaps where the pharmaceuticals were produced? He heard a crashing sound, like two aluminum saucepans being struck together. But he knew not to trust his ears. That could be anything from a fire alarm to…gunfire.

He peered through the window. Someone was running straight down the line of shiny production machines and in his direction. The figure ran hunched over, staying low.

He stepped back as one of the large double doors eased open, flattening against the wall as a small hand appeared, then the person crept through, staying low and moving silently.

He grabbed the wrist and pulled, throwing the intruder against the bank of windows with a thump. Air hissed out of her lungs. He looked down at the startled face of Paige Morris, her mouth open and about to scream, but she hesitated as recognition lifted her features.

He angled his head and kissed her on the lips. This was not a brief peck of recognition, but the hard, possessive contact of a man finding his woman. If they made it out of here, he was going to tell her that he loved her and ask her again to be his wife.

She had almost been once. He wanted that again. It was why he had thrown her from the sled into deep drifting snow. And it was why he had told her not to come back here. Yet, here she was.

Logan drew back. "I told you to stay away from here."

"He's coming." Paige pointed back the way she had come.

"Who?"

"Sinclair."

He pulled her farther from the door, putting himself between it and her.

"Who's Sinclair?" he asked.

"Production manager. He has a gun. Chasing me." Her words were tortured with the efforts of her breathing as she broke into sobs. She clung to his free arm with both hands. "I'm so glad to see you. I was so afraid. I thought... Oh, Logan, those men."

"Lost them in the woods."

She sobbed. "I'm so sorry about everything. That I hurt you. I never meant to hurt you."

"Later, Paige."

He set her aside. A moment later her pursuer led through the door with his gun. Logan snatched it from him and had the pleasure of seeing the surprise register on his face before he used the butt end of the man's weapon to knock Sinclair unconscious.

"Now *he* has a head injury," said Logan, looking at the downed man. Then he turned to Paige. "That Sinclair?"

"Yes." She tugged on his arm to draw his attention back to her. "Logan, there are three more of them on the loading dock. They're my colleagues. My new supervisor, the CFO and our head of security."

"Lou?" He shook his head. "Can't believe it."

"The sheriff got shot. That was him we saw fall. His shoulder, I think. He's still on his feet. But Logan, Sinclair shot Drake twice. He's in shipping, and Hockings and the sheriff are on the loading dock. The others have them pinned.

"Who has the keys to the DHS agent's vehicle?"

"Hockings was driving."

Logan nodded. "Without their truck, that SUV is their way out. They'll need to kill them if they plan to use their vehicle."

"But Hockings says the box truck is empty," said Paige. "And I found the shipment. It's in boxes, twelve of twelve, right through there in shipping." She pointed in the direction she had come.

"Let's go." Logan stood and checked Sinclair's weapon. The clip had been fired, but he had eight rounds left.

Paige was beside him, clinging to his coat as they crept across the filling floor area and through the double doors to shipping.

"That's them," she said, pointing at the innocuous boxes.

"What's inside?" he asked.

"A painful death," she said, her gaze lingering on the packages.

Logan pointed to the blood trail.

"That's where I left Drake," she whispered.

"He's hiding, probably."

"Go after him?" she asked.

He shook his head and then glanced toward the loading dock. Drake would have to wait.

They paused at the doors, peering through the reinforced glass to the loading dock.

Paige gasped. Lou Reber stood over the sheriff and Agent Hockings. The pair were both down and the sheriff had his hand on Hockings chest, pressing hard.

"She's been shot," whispered Logan.

Behind Reber stood Vitale, aiming her weapon at the downed pair as she looked about.

"Where's Sinclair?" she asked. "And where is that meddlesome splinter of a woman?"

Logan spared her a grin. "That's you."

"Sinclair went after her, through there," said Newman, motioning her pistol toward the doors behind which they stood. She and Logan ducked.

"Lou, get the boxes and load them into the SUV. Carol, get the keys."

Logan and Paige moved quickly to a position just beyond the boxes reaching cover as Lou Reber entered the room, weapon up and eyes alert. This one, Logan thought, knows how to use his weapon.

Logan hit him low and hard. Reber sprawled backward, the weapon going up. Reber hit the concrete on his back with Logan on top of him. Logan grabbed the wrist holding the gun as the head of security tried to bring the weapon to position.

"What was that?" The voice came from the dock.

"Go see," said Veronica.

Logan drew back his left arm and swung. The uppercut snapped Lou's head back. The crack told Logan that he'd broken the man's jaw. Behind him, the door opened.

He turned to see Carol Newman frozen in the doorway, mouth hanging open and weapon drooping.

Paige darted into his peripheral vision. She had Carol's wrist in both of her hands as she continued to run, diving now and sweeping Carol along with her as the two toppled.

Reber lay inert on his back, his jaw now at an unnatural angle as Logan rose to his feet.

"What's happening?" shouted Veronica. Then came a gunshot and silence. Logan waited for Paige and Carol Newman to come to a stop. He wasn't surprised to see Paige on top, Carol's gun beside them and both of Carol's arms pinned to the floor.

"Let me up," said Carol, her eyes bloodshot as she spit the words.

Logan collected her gun and nodded to Paige. Carol made a great show of slowly rising. Logan stepped back so that when Carol made the lunge at him, he easily sidestepped. Paige was up now, too, and holding a mop like a Louisville Slugger. She swung, hitting Carol across the back. Carol sprawled on the concrete beside Lou.

"That's for suspending me," said Paige, *"for doing my job."*

Logan handed her a pistol and the two moved to the loading dock window.

Beyond, they saw that Rylee was still down, but so was Vitale. The sheriff, his arm dripping blood, held Vitale's weapon. One look at the woman's ruined face and motionless body told Paige that the CFO of Rathburn-Bramley was dead.

Logan shouted to the sheriff. "Trace! It's Constable Lynch and Paige Morris. Sinclair is unconscious and Newman is down."

"They shot Rylee," he said, his voice tortured.

"Permission to come in."

"Yes."

"What about her?" asked Paige, pointing at Newman who had pushed up to her arms, looking like a woman struggling with a yoga pose.

Logan handed Paige Newman's weapon and then stooped. In a moment he'd levered Newman onto his shoulder and was heading back to the door. Paige pushed it open for him and then followed behind him.

Logan lay Newman beside Vitale and pointed the handgun at her head. Carol stopped moving.

"Watch her," said Logan and then he disappeared, returning with Drake over his shoulder and dragging Lou Reber's inert body by one ankle. He left Reber on the opposite side of Vitale from Newman. Drake, he gently set down beside Hockings. Drake groaned and curled to his side; his hands coated with his blood.

"Dead?" asked Trace, motioning to Lou.

"Unconscious."

Trace gave the downed man a critical stare and then nodded. Logan removed his coat and stripped off his jacket before replacing his coat. Then he folded the polar fleece into a pad and pressed it to Allen Drake's bleeding middle.

Logan then took over watching their adversaries and Paige checked the DHS agent. She knelt beside Hockings and drew back the woman's coat. Her dark sweater was soaked and glistening with blood.

"Caught two in my vest, but one got under my arm," Hockings said. Her voice was weak and her color gray. "Lung is punctured."

"I'll get the EMS. They're on the road with the truck."

She tried her phone but the call failed. Logan held out the key to the snowmobile.

"Go get help," said Sheriff Trace. "Tell them we've neutralized the enemy."

Logan kept his gun raised and aimed at the three captured members of Siming's Army. "I parked it out front behind the shrubs."

She hesitated only a moment and then snatched the key and ran through the doors and out of sight.

She was not gone long, returning with Mr. Garrett, who carried his bag over his shoulder like Santa Claus.

"The state police are on the way," she said. "Came over the radio in the fire truck."

"Thank God," said Trace, who had been keeping steady pressure on Hockings's wound. Despite his efforts, her skin had taken on a gray tone and her breathing was shallow.

"Fire truck is standing by with the box truck and they said to tell you the EMS vehicle is functional but stranded."

The sheriff scowled. "She needs a hospital."

Drake was no longer groaning. Garrett went to Drake first, checking his vitals. Then he lifted Drake's shirt. Logan saw two tiny black holes above his belly button.

They oozed blood steadily. Garrett cleaned and bandaged the wound.

The loading dock was freezing. Snow blew in through the open bay door and swirled around them. Paige went to the sheriff and DHS agent, who were on the opposite side of the open bay door from the captives. She spoke in quiet tones, so as not to be heard by Newman, whom Paige was not certain was semiconscious. Logan stood over the captives, weapon out and ready.

"What should we do with the shipment?" asked Paige to Rylee.

Rylee looked up at her.

"Secure it or destroy it?"

"Secure for forensics," Rylee whispered.

Mr. Garrett was completing his triage of Allen Drake and was now checking the vitals on Reber, pressing two fingers to the vessels at his neck.

"The pathogen isn't safe on the shipping floor," Paige said to Trace. "If any more of that group gets here, they'll find it. I need to move it."

"We should pour the stuff down the drain," said the sheriff.

"That won't kill a virus. It will only release it."

"So where are we taking it?" asked Trace.

She thought about that. If the backup that arrived first was from Siming's Army instead of the federal government, they would search the warehouse.

"I don't know. I'd prefer to lock it up," said Paige.

"Not here," said Hockings, the words causing her such pain, sweat popped out on her forehead.

"It's got to be somewhere they won't know to look," said Trace. "I'm hoping that the cavalry is coming. But in this storm, it's a crap shoot. Siming's Army could get here first. Paige is right. We need to do something with those boxes."

Paige understood. Hockings was down. Sheriff Trace was injured. She motioned to Logan, calling him to them. He cast a glance to Newman and then left that side of the dock to kneel beside Paige. But his attention remained fixed on his captives while Paige explained the situation.

His restless gaze flicked to her and then back across the loading dock.

"What's in those boxes might get us killed. Think about Lori," he said. "What would happen to her if something happens to us?"

That fired off angry sparks inside her. "I *am* thinking of her. If anyone breaks even one of those containers and the virus escapes, it could infect our entire village."

"Bury it out in the snow?" suggested Logan.

"Cold won't kill a virus." They faced off. "Do you have an idea or not?"

Logan dropped his gaze and nodded. "Firehouse has a locking freezer."

The sheriff glanced to Hockings, who nodded her permission and then gritted her teeth against the pain. Her breathing was shallow and her lips blue.

"How?" asked the sheriff.

"Use the snowmobile," said Logan. "Make a sled."

"Out of what?" asked Paige.

"Tarp will do," said Logan.

"The snowmobile will leave a trail," said Trace.

"One they can't follow with a car or truck," countered Logan.

"If that tarp rips or one of those boxes breaks open, it's all over. I am not loading a virulent, deadly pathogen onto a tarp."

"It can't be here if they get here first," said the sheriff.

Conversation ceased as Garrett crossed the windy portion of concrete that separated his triage patients and set his bag beside Agent Hockings. He and the sheriff were carefully removing the agent's vest to reach the wound.

Garrett pointed at Trace's hand with his scissors. "Whose blood is that?"

"Mine."

"You're shot, too?"

The sheriff grimaced. "Focus on her."

Garrett slipped Hockings's clothing up to expose the sucking wound under her armpit. Then he retrieved a plastic bag from his medical kit and placed it over the wound. The sucking sound ceased. Hockings smiled as if that bag gave her some relief. Garrett taped the bag in place and then removed the coat from Hockings's arm and wrapped a blood pressure cuff around her biceps. In a few moments he looked up from his blood pressure gauge. His voice was calm as he spoke to Logan. "I need to get her and Drake to the EMS vehicle now."

"Snowmobile," said Logan. Then he stilled. "But can she stay on the seat?"

The sheriff shook his head as Hockings nodded that she could.

Paige gestured to Drake, lying motionless on his back heedless of the blowing snow. "He can't."

"I have a rigid spine board on the truck," said Garrett. "We could get it and use it for you," he said to Agent Hockings. "Then we can use it for Drake. I have two beds there."

"How big is that board?" asked Logan.

"Seven feet by about two feet. Made of hard plastic and it has multiple nylon straps to hold the patient. I've never used it as a sled, but it would work."

Logan, Paige and the sheriff exchanged glances.

"Yes, that would work," said the sheriff.

"I'll take them," said Paige.

"After I secure the prisoners, I'll get the boxes ready," said Logan.

"You know which ones?" she asked.

"You showed me."

She nodded and headed out. He went back to guarding his captives. A few minutes later she was zipping effortlessly across the empty lot, over the curb that had vanished under the nine inches of heavy wet snow. She glided to a stop beside the fire truck.

She returned with Mrs. Unger, who offered to help at the loading dock. Unger held a rope fixed to the spine board as Paige retraced her course riding back. There she discovered that Newman and Reber had their ankles and wrists duct-taped. Newman sat up, hands behind her back, glaring at them. A strip of tape also covered her mouth.

"She has a bigger vocabulary of curse words than any marine that I have ever met," said Logan by way of explanation. "I'm moving them off the loading dock and out of the cold."

Logan carried Hockings down from the loading dock steps as the longtime principal stood over her prisoners, gun in hand, like an aged Annie Oakley.

They strapped the DHS agent, wrapped in a blanket, to the improvised sled. Garrett sat behind Paige on the snowmobile as Paige went slow, but the blanket was thoroughly snow covered when they reached the volunteers, who immediately moved Hockings to the EMS vehicle, board and all.

"I wonder if she and the sheriff have a thing?" asked Paige.

"Engaged," said Garrett and stepped off the sled.

"Wedding is in January. That is if I can get enough fluids into her to keep her blood pressure from crashing and if we can get her to the medical facility and if she doesn't get an infection."

"I'll say a prayer," said Paige.

The moment the volunteers returned the spine board, Paige was on her way to collect Drake. She found Unger watching the prisoners as Logan was in the shipping area getting the boxes ready. Paige and the sheriff helped Drake down the stairs to the spine board. Once her patient was secured and the sheriff seated behind her, they headed back again to the road.

When they reached the EMS vehicle, the crew collected Drake from the makeshift sled. The sheriff stepped off the back of the snowmobile and leaned in, speaking just loud enough for her to hear over the motor and howling wind.

"Get those boxes out of here," he said.

Paige left the volunteer corps, their vehicles stranded in the snow until the plows arrived. At least Hockings and Drake had the EMS vehicle. Ironic that the representatives who shot them had also been instrumental in purchasing the equipment that might save their lives.

Paige sped back toward the loading dock. Garrett had his mission. She had hers.

Chapter Twenty-Five

If anything, the snow had gotten heavier, changing from the thick white blobs that had been cascading down the entire day to stinging needles of ice. Already, the change was adding a crusty layer over the packing snow.

Paige returned to Logan, her clothing now drenched and her teeth chattering. She knew she needed to warm up, get out of her wet things, but there was no time.

Unger greeted her and ushered her past the dead body of Veronica Vitale, now covered with a blanket.

"Logan moved the prisoners inside to the filling floor."

Unger led the way past a bundle of the twelve boxes on the loading dock, now secured together with plastic wrap. At the base, he had used a tarp and packing tape until it formed a rectangle of six boxes stacked two high and approximately five feet long. The resulting grouping was slightly wider and shorter than the spine board. She glanced at the visible packing numbers and recognized a match.

Paige followed the school principal through shipping and into the filling floor. There Logan stood watch over Reber, Sinclair and Newman, all now secured to the conveyers with electrical tape. In this area, the captives were out of the cold.

Unger drew up a chair. "This will be easy."

Not if Siming's Army got here first, thought Paige, but said nothing.

At the loading dock, Paige paused to glance back the way they had come.

"Should we bring Unger? I don't like to leave her."

"I asked her that. She said she's staying."

"She understands that the police might not get here first?"

Logan nodded. "She knows. Unger told me to get this out of here as Agent Hockings instructed."

"All right."

They carried the load down the steps with the care they would have exercised if it had held a baby. Logan used the ropes provided by the volunteers to fix the board to the back of the snowmobile and they were underway, with Logan driving and her watching the sled to be certain it did not overturn.

The ride was slow, with Logan picking his way through the dark. Visibility was terrible but she thought the change in snow from light to icy might signal the end of the storm.

They headed away from the volunteers and the plant, taking the route through the park to the fire station. As they reached Main Street, Logan paused, idling.

"What?" she asked, looking around at the empty street and the icy mix falling through the beams of the street-lights.

"Plowed," he said.

She looked up the snowy road to Main Street and the distinctive piles of snow that told her that the highway department had finally reached them. That meant the state police would be here soon.

"What do we do?" she asked.

"Keep going." He set them in motion, pulling into the fire station.

Logan parked along the building to the side entrance and used the key.

"You volunteer?" she asked.

"Constable gets a key." He sent her inside to raise the bay door as he moved the load. She found the remote button. The garage-style doors lifted as Logan drew up out front. Beyond him a luxury SUV with chains, skidding and fishtailing down the road, came to a graceless stop just past the drive of the station.

Logan flicked off the motor. "That's Connor."

He stood beside the snowmobile, eying his brother as he approached.

"Paige's mom is worried," said Connor. "Said you took her to the factory hours ago."

"How'd you find us?" asked Logan.

"Spotted the snowmobile headlight from Main Street. I was heading to the factory, but I took a chance."

Connor waded through the snow to the tread tracks of his snowmobile as Paige's skin began to prickle. Was he here to help or...

"What's that?" asked Connor, pausing before the blue tarp.

"I was asked to secure this until the state police arrive."

"Why?"

"It's something dangerous."

"Let's go," said Connor, grabbing one side.

Logan hesitated a moment, glancing to her. Then he took the other side and they brought the load into the garage. Once there Connor took out his phone and placed a call.

"You have service?" asked Paige.

He nodded. "Just came back on a few minutes ago."

Then he spoke into the phone. "Yeah, I found them. We're at the fire station on Turkey Hollow Road." A pause. "Yeah. Safe and sound. Great." He disconnected the call.

Paige watched Connor tuck away his phone. Something didn't sit right. She squinted, thinking, and then it came to her. She'd heard Connor speak to his father on the phone many times. He always ended the call with the same thing.

I love you, Dad.

But not this time. So who had he really called?

Paige was about to close the door, but instead she watched Connor as he glared at Logan with a look she had never seen before. It was…hatred.

A chill went down her spine and her hand froze on the button. She'd been right to suspect Connor. He was guilty of far more than drugging her, lying to her.

"Logan?"

Connor stepped back, glaring at her as he retrieved a pistol from his coat and aimed it at Logan.

"Step over there, Logan."

Logan's smile dropped and his hands raised.

"Connor. Don't shoot Paige. We won't stop you."

"I won't. But I should." He glowered at her through bloodshot eyes. "I did this for you. That house. Bringing that company here. Everything. But it wasn't enough, was it? You still wanted him!"

Paige stared in horror as if watching a car crash. She could not seem to look away. Connor turned his glare and his gun on Logan. She couldn't breathe.

"You aren't good enough for her. You know that, don't you?"

"Always have," said Logan.

Logan backed away from the boxes, moving toward her.

"They're coming and they won't stop until they get this," said Connor.

"You can't let them," said Paige.

"I can."

She glanced toward the open bay door. Help was coming, she realized, but not fast enough.

Chapter Twenty-Six

Paige looked out at the snowy road. She was shivering again, in her wet clothing. Her fingers were so stiff. She flexed them, trying to get the blood flowing again.

A large vehicle trundled down Main, stopping at the turn at the top of the hill.

"Hummer," said Logan. "That's how they got through."

"Who are they?" she asked.

"Siming's Army," said Connor, lowering his gun. "I've done everything they've asked. But not this. I won't kill you, but they will. You need to go. Now."

Logan turned to her, extending his hand. "Come on."

She shook her head. "They'll take the virus. They'll use it. That could kill thousands." She turned to Connor, pleading. "Connor, help us."

He snorted and shook his head.

"Logan, we have to try. Close the door. Hold them, slow them, until the state police get here."

He smiled at her. She could not understand the expression. It looked like admiration.

"This is the hill on which you are prepared to die?" asked Logan.

She nodded, but the shivering made it seem an involuntary tremor. She lifted her hand and pushed the button to close the bay door.

"Do you trust me?"

"Yes."

"Then come with me."

He held out his hand and she did not hesitate, clasping tight and running with him out the side door on stiff legs and feet so cold she stumbled along, clumsy as she tried to keep pace. She heard the chains on the Hummer slow and then go silent. Vehicle doors opened and slammed. The bay door rattled up.

Logan was not a coward. He must have a plan, some way to stop them once they had the boxes.

She and Logan crept behind the building. He led them toward Main, wading through deep snow down the hill to the river and then up the steep bank toward the bridge.

What were they doing?

The wind burned her skin. She lowered her chin so her face was pressed to his back as she struggled along, hoping she had not just made the mistake that might end the lives of everyone she knew and loved.

No. She trusted Logan.

They reached the bridge that crossed onto Main and stepped from the deep snow onto the plowed, salted surface. She shivered continuously as they made their way east toward his offices and the road that crossed back over the river and down to the factory.

What was their destination? She wanted to ask but was so tired she could barely walk let alone speak.

Down Main Street came the flashing of red-and-blue lights. Three state police vehicles, salt-stained and flecked with mud, appeared behind a large plow. The caravan reached them and stopped.

Detective Albritton stepped out and into the snowbank. Logan was already striding in the officer's direction.

"Constable Lynch?" said Albritton.

"Where is the biohazard?"

Paige glanced back the way they had come. Had the men taken the boxes? If the terrorists reached Main, they could head west. Were they driving away with the pathogen right now or, worse yet, had they opened one of those boxes?

She straightened, noticing that she had stopped shivering and now felt pleasantly warm. But she still couldn't feel her toes or hands. She lifted her arm to point, like a retriever, toward their target.

"It's at the factory," said Logan.

She gaped at him.

He smiled down at her. "I sliced the bottom of each box and switched out the contents while you were getting help for Hockings and Trace."

Logan switched the boxes?

Confusion made her question difficult to compose.

"What... What's back there?" she asked, stammering.

"I'm not sure. Air freshener?"

That wasn't right. She shook her head with slow deliberation. "We don't make that. Dis-disinfectant spray?"

"Maybe." He was looking at her oddly.

"S-smart," she whispered.

Was it her imagination, or did she sound drunk right now?

"You knew Connor was..."

"There for the boxes? Yes. But I hoped I was wrong."

She realized then that Logan had tested his brother, let him take the boxes and trusted he wouldn't kill them both. Paige didn't know if she should be angry or admiring. But he'd switched the contents without telling her. Kept it from her. She lowered her head as shame and understanding collided. This is how she'd made him feel.

"Constable Lynch," said Albritton, "we need you to

take us to the contents of those boxes. I've got DHS right behind us and some very scary folks from the CDC."

The Centers for Disease Control was here? Thank God, she thought. She was hot now and struggled to drop off her gloves and then fumbled with her zipper.

Mr. Garrett waded through the snowdrift to them. Logan identified him to the police.

"I've got three gunshot victims down there," said Garrett. "I need that road plowed so we can get through."

The plow was redirected to clear Raquette Road.

"Agent Hockings? Where is she?" asked Albritton.

"Both Agent Hockings and the sheriff are down there in my EMS vehicle with the CEO, Allen Drake, but they need to be on their way to Plattsville Medical." Mr. Garrett flicked on a pen light and shone it in Paige's face. "And that's where you are going, as well, Dr. Morris. You've got frostbite and I think you are hypothermic." He pointed to her cheeks.

She shook her head. "No. I'm hot," she said, pulling off her cap.

Garrett pulled it back in place. "Logan. Get her inside right now."

"He's coming with us to the warehouse," said Albritton.

Logan gave Paige a long look and then turned to Mr. Garrett.

"You'll see to her?"

"Yes. Of course."

Garrett helped her walk down to a state police vehicle. "Wait here," he told her.

The interior was stiflingly hot. In a few minutes she was loaded into an empty EMS vehicle. Drake, Hockings and Trace, she was told, were already in transit aboard a different ambulance. There the volunteers had stripped

Paige out of every stitch of clothing. She was wet right down to her underthings. And her fingers were puckered and a ghastly, ghostly gray.

"That isn't good," she said.

Paige didn't remember much of the trip to the medical center. She'd been bundled in blankets. Under her, they used a blanket filled with warm air. It sounded like a hair dryer blowing in her ear the entire way to Plattsville.

"I'm thirsty," she said to Mr. Garrett.

"I know. But you can't drink anything until you see the doctor."

Chapter Twenty-Seven

Logan got the CDC to the right set of boxes. They wore yellow outfits that looked more suited to a moonwalk than a pickup, but they gathered all the deadly pathogens produced at the plant.

He called home as soon as he had a minute and got Mrs. Morris. He explained what had happened. She asked several questions as to Paige's location and condition. Then he heard her shout for Lori and hung up on him.

A bit later he ran into Detective Albritton in the shipping area and asked about Connor. The detective told him that the men from Siming's Army had taken the decoy boxes and left his brother behind. Connor was now in federal custody and Logan could not see him.

Logan went back to work for much of the night, assisting federal and local law enforcement. Detective Albritton tracked him down after midnight and told him that he had a condition report on Paige.

"The medical center treated her for hypothermia and frostbite. They will keep her at least until tomorrow."

"Will she be all right?" asked Logan.

"She's going to be fine. The hypothermia was the most dangerous part. Frostbite was minor. But they got her all warmed up."

He was so relieved he slid down the warehouse wall

right to the floor. Was this how it had been for her, hearing he had been injured and fearing the worst?

For that moment he had just an inkling of what he had put her through, reenlisting, going into a combat zone and then the brain injury. No wonder she'd been cautious of resuming a relationship with him. He had not listened to her. Had not considered her feelings or desires. In different circumstances, he might have done the same as she had. Since they'd taken Paige, fear had been so bad, he could barely function, and she'd been only half a county away.

"What was I thinking?" he asked himself. Young and dumb, his father had called him. That he had been.

Logan got home well past midnight to find his father waiting. Lori and her grandmother had headed to the medical center to see Paige. Steven and Valerie were in bed.

Logan sat with his father in the kitchen where all important matters were discussed. Then he explained to his dad everything that had happened. When he told him what Connor had done, his dad listened in grim-faced silence. When Logan told him that his older son had been arrested by the FBI, his father did something Logan had not seen since the death of his mother.

His dad started to cry. Logan wrapped his arms about his dad as he watched another piece of his father's heart break away.

It was a long time before the two headed upstairs to their rooms.

After checking on Valerie and Steven, both asleep, Logan showered and headed back to the factory. The FBI had arrived, and both FBI and DHS agents were removing computers and boxes of files from Rathburn-

Bramley. They took a statement from him and then told him to go home and get some sleep.

He headed back up the hill on roads that were freshly plowed and sanded. Beyond the graying piles of snow left by the plows, the world lay under a deep blanket of unbroken white.

Instead of going home, Logan headed to Plattsville Medical Center to find that Lori and Mrs. Morris had left some time ago. He checked in on Paige, still in the ER but sleeping. They let him speak to her. She gave him a smile and asked if he was okay. She looked exhausted, so he let her sleep, returning home to his own bed as the sun was rising.

He woke a few hours later and called the medical center. Paige was now in a room. Another call to Paige's mother's cell, and he learned from her mother that Paige was with the doctor and would be home tomorrow. Her mother reported that FBI agents were also there, waiting to speak to Paige.

Running on coffee and three hours' sleep, Logan faced Friday and the circus of law enforcement streaming in and out of his little village. He finally got a call back from Child Protective Services about fostering the Sullivan kids and the correct paperwork via email attachment. His dad told him that Paige had returned home and they had been assigned protection. He tried to get home to see them, but the day was eaten up by the needs of others.

Albritton checked in and told him they'd made some major arrests. Thanks to him and to Paige, they had shut down an entire sleeper cell of the terrorist organization. This cell of Siming's Army was responsible for pickup and dissemination of the virus. Each member had been immunized against the contagion, and Albritton said they got them all.

By the time he made it home on Friday night, the kids were all asleep, Paige and her mom were also in bed and only his dad was up waiting for him.

"Funeral tomorrow," said his dad. "Ten a.m."

"How are Steven and Valerie?"

"They had a lot of questions about what will happen tomorrow. I was honest." His dad also looked exhausted. This situation had taken a heavy toll on them all.

"How do you prepare children for something like this?" said Logan.

"I don't know. I don't really think that you can."

SATURDAY, THE BLACK limo carried them all the short distance to the church for services. The Sullivans looked stunned as the two coffins holding their parents were paraded down the center aisle of the Methodist church. Services were performed and then they all piled back into the limo to be driven to the cemetery. Despite the snow, the ground was not frozen. The artificial green grass draped the fresh grave over which two coffins were now suspended. The kids clung to Paige as the minister spoke of loss and hope and love. None of it made sense to Logan. He could only imagine what Valarie and Steven were feeling. Logan thought of his mother, taken too soon, and of her funeral and the day he'd worn his first black suit.

The somber scene changed when they reached the Lynches' house, now filled with food and light. The ladies from the Methodist church had taken over the house, adding folding chairs, flowers and food…so much food.

Lori stood with Steven and Valerie, following Paige and Mr. Lynch's example of greeting all guests. The entire village appeared to be here, gathered to chat and offer sympathy and support. Logan was speaking with the minister when Paige came to get him and drew him out to the back porch.

"What's wrong?" he asked.

She motioned to the two small figures sitting alone at the picnic table in the backyard in the snow. Steven and Valerie hunched side by side on the tabletop, feet resting on the icy seat. They were still in their funeral garb but wearing their brightly colored snow coats over them. They were uncharacteristically still.

"Steven wants to talk to you," said Paige.

Logan and Paige hurried out to speak to the pair. Paige pushed away the snow from the table and then sat beside Steven. Logan rounded the table and flanked Valerie, resting one foot on the bench.

"Hi, Steven. What's going on?" said Logan.

The boy turned to him with red-rimmed eyes. "I'm a jinx."

"You're what?"

"A jinx. My dad got run over and killed and then my mom made a mistake with those pills and died. Then we moved in here and—" he looked at Paige "—your house burned down. Then you had to go to the hospital." He ended with a wail. "And it's all my fault!"

Paige gathered him in. "None of this is your fault."

At her brother's tears, Valerie began to sob. It was the first time he'd seen them cry, really cry, since all this tragedy had begun.

Logan picked Valerie up and sat beside Steven, rocking the girl as the sobs shook her. Both he and Paige let them cry, making sounds of comfort as they held tight.

Finally, the weeping slowed to occasional sniffing and the swipe of a mitten over a tear-stained cheek.

"Now, you think this is your fault, Steven, but I'm going to tell you the truth," said Logan. "None of this was an accident or due to bad luck. This all happened for a reason, and your dad is a hero. He found out something, something really, really bad happening at his work. And he tried to tell someone, but some bad people found out and they didn't want him to tell. It was not an accident. They hit him on purpose, Steven, but even after he was hit by that vehicle, he did the right thing and told Paige about it and she told me. Your father saved the lives of many, many people."

Steven stared with wide eyes as Paige took over and told them both about their dad and how their mom died because she knew the secret the bad men didn't want anyone to know. She told them all of it in terms he thought they would understand. About the virus and the men who were after it and how Logan tricked them and how they got away. When she was done they stared at her as if she'd gone crazy.

"My parents died to save all those people?" asked Steven.

"Yes. I know it's not fair, but they were protecting both of you and me and everyone in this entire village. Your dad figured it out. He was the first one to figure out what was happening."

Logan didn't know if this made the loss easier because there was no easy way to lose your parents.

"I'm not a jinx," he said, staring at the ground now, and speaking to himself.

"You are not," Paige said. "You are brave, like your father and kind like your mother and smart like both of them."

He nodded, and Logan hoped Steven believed her, because it was true.

"They would never have left you. They were taken from us all by bad people," said Paige.

"Are they in jail?" asked Valerie.

Logan took that one. "Every one of them, and they will stay there, too. Come on, you two, let's go back inside."

Valerie hesitated. "Sammy Begley says we have to go to an orphanage now because our aunt ran away and we have no parents. He said we're orphans, just like Annie."

Logan felt the stab of grief at the pain inflicted on this pair. He dropped to his knee beside Valerie.

"We are looking for your aunt. Until we speak to her, you are staying with me. I want you both to stay with me."

Valerie looked up at him through wet, spiky lashes and threw herself against him and held on for dear life.

"Really?" she said into the collar of his coat.

"Yes. I want you both with all my heart," he said.

Logan hugged the little girl, lifting her to his hip. Paige wrapped an arm around Steven. Normally too old for this sort of display of emotion, he leaned his head against her as they headed toward the house.

"Can we go upstairs?" asked Valerie.

"Of course," said Paige.

They walked the two into the house and up to the room the kids currently shared. After closing the door, Logan turned to Paige.

"I spoke to Child Welfare on getting permanent custody," said Logan. "I've started the paperwork."

She nodded.

"What do you think?" he asked.

"I think Valerie and Steven are very lucky to have someone like you in their lives. But I'm sure Freda will take custody," she said, speaking of the children's aunt.

"Then why isn't she here?" he asked.

Paige gave him a bewildered look. "I don't know."

"I'm thinking about having them see someone," said Logan. "A therapist, I mean."

"That seems wise."

His father called up the stairs to Logan.

"Logan, you two got a minute? The sheriff is here."

Chapter Twenty-Eight

Sheriff Trace, Logan and Paige stepped out onto the front porch, which was the only place not overflowing with guests.

The sheriff had his arm in a sling from the bullet that had grazed his biceps. Fourteen stitches later, he was discharged, but his fiancée, Agent Hockings, had been transferred to Glens Falls Hospital.

"How is Agent Hockings?" asked Logan.

He knew only that, unlike Paige, Hockings's condition was serious.

"Stable. Still in the ICU. The bullet traveled from her armpit through a major artery there." The sheriff lifted his arm and pointed to the place where the bullet had missed her body armor and struck flesh. "It hit a rib on the way in, slowed it down and redirected it away from her heart. Thank God. But the bullet did puncture her lung. She's had surgery to stop the bleeding and remove the bullet. That chunk of lead made it between two ribs in her back and then stopped. Doctor said it sat just under the skin in her back below the shoulder blade."

"She going to be all right?" asked Paige.

"She's battling an infection. Winning. She'll make it. I've never met a stronger woman."

But Logan had. He'd met Paige.

"How are you feeling, Dr. Morris?" asked the sheriff.

"They released me yesterday. Now I'm just tired."

"That's good news." The pleasantries ended and the sheriff began an update. He'd been in contact with both Detective Albritton and Hockings's supervisor.

According to Trace, Reber, Newman and Park were all in federal custody. The box truck driver had been apprehended, along with the two gunmen who had chased him and Paige on snowmobiles. One had shattered his hip, the other had frostbite from trying to walk out on a broken ankle after his snowmobile was destroyed in the fall from the bridge. They were members of a sleeper cell of Siming's Army. One of the two was cooperating with authorities. He reported that Siming's Army had recruited several employees of Rathburn-Bramley, including the CFO and the head of security.

"Why would the CFO of that company work with terrorists?" asked Logan.

"Money. A lot of it. Nearly a half million dollars that they know about so far. She appears to be the first one up here to be on their payroll."

"And the others?" asked Paige.

"Well, Sullivan wasn't. He's the one who discovered they were producing something off the books and reported it to Reber. Unfortunately, your head of security has a wife with a chronic back injury."

Paige knew that. "Skiing accident. She's had two surgeries."

"And she has an opioid addiction. Mr. Reber was caught stealing product and, instead of firing him, Vitale put him on the payroll and supplied his wife with drugs," said Trace. "Oh, I almost forgot. Reber was the driver who killed Dr. Edward Sullivan."

Logan straightened at this revelation. "How do you know?"

"Confessed. A buddy, now on suspension in Poughkeepsie, found him a guy up here with a possession conviction and a DUI, a perfect fall guy. Lou stole his vehicle and waited in that vehicle for Sullivan to take his run. Reber claims he hit Sullivan and left him to die. Then he returned the truck and made it back to Rathburn-Bramley before his shift."

"You have evidence to back that up?" asked Logan.

"We will. We've impounded the vehicle. We're hopeful we'll get something solid."

"This was all for his wife?" asked Paige in disbelief.

"That's right." There was a pause in the conversation. Trace held Logan's gaze a moment, making him wonder if Trace was also contemplating what they each would or wouldn't do for their women.

"What about Carol Newman?" asked Paige, mentioning the new supervisor who had shot at them on the loading dock.

"When Vitale came on the payroll, she hired a new personnel director. The new personnel director does not seem connected except that he hired anyone that Vitale told him to. When she said to hire Carol Newman, a woman with zero knowledge or experience in pharmaceuticals, he did just that. Newman is one of Siming's Army. So is Sinclair Park, the production manager. He had experience in production, but he's one of them, too."

"Who set the fire?" asked Logan.

"We believe that was also Reber or Park. Again, made to look like you did it, Paige. You were not supposed to survive to contradict their narrative."

"How long will we have the FBI protection?" asked

Paige, glancing to the agents parked in the SUV in the driveway.

"At least until they shut down this organization. Hard to say. They're making arrests."

Logan glanced toward the house. "You know that I'm fostering Steven and Valerie Sullivan."

"I'm aware," said Trace.

"I've applied for permanent placement until they find their aunt. Do you have information on her whereabouts?"

"Oh, yes. I do. DHS found her," said Trace. "She's working with them. When she discovered her sister's body, she ran. Apparently, her sister wouldn't even take an aspirin. Objected to medications in general, I was told."

"I said from the beginning that she would not have taken her life," said Paige.

"Or taken those pills to sleep, apparently." Trace absently rubbed his knuckles over the stubble on his jaw. "Ms. Kubr's sister told her things, a lot of things. Everything that her husband told her. According to Detective Albritton, Kubr believed they'd kill her, too, so she ran."

"Understandable. But her niece and nephew. When is she coming back?" asked Paige.

"She's requested witness protection. FBI is turning her over to the Marshals Services. Albritton doesn't think they'll take her, but he did say that she was in no condition to take over custody. I think you'd be the better choice."

Trace nodded.

"She's willing to give up custody claims?" asked Paige, incredulous.

"That's what I was told by the FBI."

"But they're her sister's children," said Paige, now bewildered.

Logan smiled. Paige would never abandon her flesh and blood and, if she had a sister, she would consider those children her children.

Logan didn't know if he should feel happy or sad that Freda didn't want custody. Happy to be able to raise those two wonderful kids, and sad at the circumstances, he supposed.

"How is Allen Drake?" asked Paige.

"He's had surgery. The bullets punctured his stomach, so infection is a worry. But his prognosis is good."

Paige smiled at this news.

Logan hesitated and then asked the tough question. "What about my brother?"

"He's in real trouble, Logan. His attorney is working out a plea bargain. It might help reduce his sentence but he's up to his neck in it. He's admitted, for instance, that he drugged Paige and that he planted those opioids on the Morrises' premises."

Paige sucked in a breath and set her jaw. She and Logan exchanged a look as her suspicion was confirmed.

"I'm sorry," she said to Logan.

"Did he tell you why?" Logan asked Trace.

"In order to plant the narcotics in her bedroom and discredit her. Having her act crazy in town right after her suspension and before they placed her under arrest made her look like she was using. Easier for them to fire her, they told him."

"But he loves Paige. How could he do that to her?"

"He claims that he didn't know about the plans for the house fire."

"But why was he working with them at all?" said Logan, the exasperation clear in his voice.

"At first, he was being blackmailed. Vitale had him investigated, along with others, looking for easy targets.

Found out he'd misappropriated village funds to pay personal debts. She had him after that. Your brother owed everybody to the tune of over $125,000. That house, the vehicles, lifestyle and his business—he didn't own any of it. I understand he didn't do well in real estate. Lost money every year."

Logan had thought his brother such a success. The reality twisted his heart and made his stomach ache. It had all been a lie. Especially the part about him looking out for his kid brother. All the time Connor had been trying to steal Paige out from under his nose. And he probably thought putting his brother in the constable's position would mean Connor would never face investigation.

That thought made her sick. Connor had underestimated Logan. He hadn't seen the improvements in his condition. Only Paige had.

Paige took Logan's hand and gave it a squeeze before drawing back. She had no siblings, but understanding reflected in her expression. Connor had betrayed them both.

"He convinced the village to hire me," Logan admitted.

"We're aware. That was one of the best and worst decisions your brother ever made. They underestimated you, Logan. I did, too, and I'm sorry about that."

"Thanks for saying so."

"I mean it, Logan. You did everything right. Switching the product, hiding the pathogen in plain sight and using the other boxes as a decoy. That was brilliant."

"What is Connor facing?" asked Logan.

"Conspiracy, fraud, embezzlement, interfering with federal investigation. Then there are the crimes against Paige, drugging her, kidnapping, planting false evidence. It's a long list. Even with a deal, he's going to federal prison, Logan. There'll be no way to avoid that. For how long will depend on how useful they find his testimony."

"I'll speak to him about that."

"That's a good idea."

"What about the men who showed up at the firehouse?" asked Paige. "Did you catch them?"

"Yes and no. FBI followed them all the way to a rest stop below Albany. They were, all four of them, squirting disinfectant spray all over the lobby and food court."

"Trying to infect travelers," said Paige. "They thought it was the pathogen."

Trace nodded and his expression grew deadly serious. "You two stopped a pandemic."

Logan let that sink in and the fallout that might now be happening if he had not made that switch.

"So instead of an epidemic unlike this country has ever seen, we have one of the cleanest rest stops on the entire New York State Thruway." He clapped Logan on the shoulder with his uninjured hand.

"But they were arrested?" asked Paige.

"Not at that time. Followed and made arrests yesterday. They led the FBI right back to their sleeper cell.

"Good work, Logan, on the switch. Really amazing work. If it were up to me, we'd get you another Medal of Honor."

Logan flushed.

"Thank you, Constable Lynch and Dr. Morris," he said with a new formality. "You two saved our lives. I know if you and Paige had not been there, Rylee and I would have died on that loading dock. We owe you and won't forget."

Now Paige was flushed.

The conversation drew to an awkward pause. The

sheriff glanced toward the road. "I'd better get back to Rylee."

Paige said her goodbyes and headed back inside as Logan walked the sheriff to his vehicle parked on the road.

"What will you do now?" asked Trace.

"I'm going to ask Paige to marry me."

The sheriff's brows lifted. "Well, best of luck with that. You two obviously make a good team."

Logan smiled. He sure hoped so. Trace extended his uninjured arm and the two shook hands.

"You ever think about running for office?" asked Trace.

"Me? What kind?" For a terrible moment he thought the sheriff was about to suggest he take over his brother's spot on the village council. He couldn't. Never.

"I think you'd be a strong candidate for sheriff of Onutake County."

Logan gaped. It took him a moment to recover. The sheriff chuckled and then slapped him on the arm.

"Think about it. You'd have my vote." Trace turned to go.

Axel Trace climbed behind the wheel and drove off. *Sheriff?* Logan shook his head. It seemed impossible. But was it?

Logan wondered what his future held. He had plans to adopt the Sullivan children and marry the mother of his child. If she'd have him, they could have more children. Lots more.

The world seemed full of possibilities. But they all hinged on whether Paige would give them a second chance.

He'd proven he could and would fight for her. He'd risked everything to save her. But that didn't mean she would marry him. She'd loved him once and he'd forgotten her. That had hurt her as much as his leaving her against her wishes. He'd made mistakes. But he was not that rash young man any longer. He was not the boy she had fallen in love with, either. And right now he was not sure if that was good or bad.

Chapter Twenty-Nine

Sunday, after church, Paige and her mother went shopping for turkey and fixings. This Thursday was Thanksgiving and they would have a full house. Logan had driven to Plattsville shopping mall for a very special piece of jewelry and had beaten the women home.

When they returned, Logan helped unload the bags of groceries. Mrs. Morris seemed out of sorts and Paige's expression was grim. Mrs. Morris took over unpacking in the kitchen while he and Paige went out to retrieve the last load. Outside, he told Paige that he had a call from someone in the Justice Department. They said that Steven and Valerie's aunt, Freda Kubr, had been accepted into witness protection.

"I sent in the paperwork for custody this morning to Child Protective Services," said Logan.

Paige gave him a worried look. "Fingers crossed."

"Because I'm male or because of this?" He lifted his fingers to his scar.

She lifted her hand and let her fingertips whisper over the scar.

"Both, really."

"Do you think I'm not capable of raising them?"

She gave him that confident smile. "I can't think of

anyone better, but bureaucracy is unpredictable. I'll be happy to help you any way I can."

That encouragement gave him hope.

"Did you find out if you can see Connor yet?"

"I'm driving my dad down to Albany tomorrow to speak to the lawyer we hired. We'll see if they let us visit him then."

"Your poor dad. First your mom and now this."

"He's taking it hard. Connor never let on that he had money troubles."

"Neither did my mom. She's only just getting out from under that bankruptcy. I still don't know why she wanted to keep that house. Well, she can't keep it now. Did I tell you she dropped the insurance?"

He didn't hide the stunned expression.

"What will she do?"

"Get something she can afford. Get a job, too, I hope. We had a fight about it in the car. I told her that I won't be moving back in with her."

"Why not?"

"It's not good for me. I told her I'd help her when I get back on my feet, but she stormed off."

"She'll get over it," he said.

Paige hoisted two of the bags and he took the rest, closing the trunk.

"Maybe. Listen, I have to help with these."

"Dad wants me to go pick up the pies he ordered from the farm stand."

"Oh, I want to come. Can you wait for me?"

"Paige, I'd wait for you…all day." Had he almost said *forever*? He would need to be braver if he was going to get through this. Funny to have a Silver Star but not be able to summon up the courage to ask the woman he loved to be his wife.

What if she said no? Worse still, what if she laughed or sneered like her mother? Paige would never laugh.

He gave her a long look as his heart walloped against his ribs. He couldn't lose her again.

"Logan, are you all right?"

"Hmm? Yes, why?"

"You look a little green." She hesitated. "I'll be ready in a few minutes."

He headed toward the living room where his father had settled into his chair to watch football. The children sprawled on the floor with their electronic devices, playing video games. Mrs. Morris and Paige were arguing in the kitchen. Paige appeared a few minutes later, red in the face.

"Ready?" she asked, holding her car keys and already in her coat.

He nodded and grabbed his jacket, realizing two things at once. First, they finally had a chance to be alone, and second, that the timing was terrible because of so many things, including the recent conflict with her mom. He was about to ask this woman to be his wife. Should he wait? But when would they next be alone? Logan didn't know what to do.

In a moment they were out the door.

"Mind if we stop at Lookout Rocks?" he asked, making his decision and committing himself to his course.

She shook her head. "I could use some serenity."

He drove them up Gunhouse Road, high above the village to the nature preserve that had a view of the entire valley. It was a beautiful spot on any day, but with the fresh layer of snow covering field and farm, it was awe inspiring.

The storm had departed, and the skies were clear blue. The air temperature was warm enough that she left her coat open as she slipped from the cab to walk through the snow to the benches set on the rocky outcropping on the crest of the hill.

"Look." She pointed toward the dark ribbon of the river. "Is that an eagle?"

She turned to find him staring at her instead of the valley. He held his smile, but it felt tight and edged with panic.

"Are you sweating?" she asked, glancing at his forehead.

"Yes. You would be, too."

She peered at him as if wondering what was amiss. "I would be? Why?"

"If you were about to ask the woman you love to marry you."

"You love?"

"Ask her again, I mean, but also for the first time."

He dropped to one knee in the snow. In his open palm was a black velvet box.

"Dr. Paige Morris, will you marry me?"

Her mouth dropped open and she blinked at him as if he had switched to a different language. Her head tilted sideways, and those blue eyes went wider and wider still.

"Oh!" was all she managed, the sound somewhere between an exhale and a groan. Then she cleared her throat. Her face had gone pink right down to her neck.

Fear and hope collided with panic and longing. He'd give her all he had if she'd just give him one more chance. And still she was speechless. Logan babbled into the ringing silence.

"I know I'm not the man I was. Everyone tells me that. But I do love you and I love Lori. You said I would be a good father. I want to be—her father, I mean."

For a man who had struggled to speak, the words certainly were flowing now, he thought.

"You're right, Logan."

He waited for the other shoe to fall, waited for her to push the ring box away and tell him to take her home. Waited for his dreams to shatter like glass thrown from this cliff to the rocks below them.

"You are not the man you once were," she said. "You're better in all the ways that matter. I'm sorry I couldn't see that sooner."

His gaze darted from their joined hands and up to those bewitching blue eyes. There he saw nothing but love and hope.

"Really?" he asked.

She brought their clasped hands to her heart. "Logan, what we had was nothing compared to what we might have. I want all of it. I love you and I want you and Lori and Steven and Valerie. I want us together as a family. We deserve each other and we deserve a fresh start."

"We do."

"I never stopped loving you," she said. "I just was afraid that you stopped loving me."

"The heart remembers even if the mind forgets." He smiled up at her. "I'm sorry this took so long. I didn't think you'd settle—"

She cut him off. "I'm not settling. I'm the luckiest woman alive. I've been given a second chance with you and I'm not going to miss this one. Yes, Logan, I will marry you and I'll be grateful to you forever for the second chance."

He opened the velvet box, presenting her with the diamond solitaire he'd chosen for her. It was a square emerald cut surrounded by smaller stones in what the jeweler called a halo-style setting. The band was platinum and had more stones flanking the central diamond. She extended her hand and he slipped the ring onto her finger.

She looped her arms around him and kissed him. He felt the love there, in her body and in that kiss. They had nearly lost each other, but had found their way back, fought to be here because this was where they were meant to be, together again.

With Lori and Steven and Valerie, they would build a family and, God willing, she would give him more children to love.

This Thanksgiving, more than any other, they had so much for which to be thankful.

* * * * *

AVAILABLE THIS MONTH FROM
Harlequin Intrigue®

SAFETY BREACH
Longview Ridge Ranch • by Delores Fossen
Former profiler Gemma Hanson is in witness protection, but she's still haunted by memories of the serial killer who tried to kill her last year. Her concerns skyrocket when Sheriff Kellan Slater tells her the murderer has learned her location and is coming to finish what he started.

UNDERCOVER ACCOMPLICE
Red, White and Built: Delta Force Deliverance
by Carol Ericson
When Delta Force soldier Hunter Mancini learns the group that kidnapped CIA operative Sue Chandler is now framing his team leader, he asks for her help. But could she be hiding something that would clear his boss?

AMBUSHED AT CHRISTMAS
Rushing Creek Crime Spree • by Barb Han
After a jogger resembling Detective Leah Cordon is murdered, rancher Deacon Kent approaches her, believing the attack is related to recent cattle mutilations. Can they find the killer before he corners Leah?

DANGEROUS CONDITIONS
Protectors at Heart • by Jenna Kernan
Former soldier Logan Lynch's first investigation as the constable of a small town leads him to microbiologist Paige Morris, whose boss was killed. Yet as they search for the murderer, Paige is forced to reveal a secret that shows the stakes couldn't be higher.

RULES IN DEFIANCE
Blackhawk Security • by Nichole Severn
Blackhawk Security investigator Elliot Dunham never expected his neighbor to show up bruised and covered in blood in the middle of the night. To protect Waylynn Hargraves, Elliot must defy the rules he's set for himself, because he knows he's all that stands between her and certain death.

HIDDEN TRUTH
Stealth • by Danica Winters
When undercover CIA agent Trevor Martin meets Sabrina Parker, the housekeeper at the ranch where he's lying low, he doesn't know she's an undercover FBI agent. After a murder on the property, the operatives must work together, but can they discover their hidden connection before it's too late?

HIATMBPA1219

INTRIGUE

Available December 17, 2019

#1899 A THREAT TO HIS FAMILY
Longview Ridge Ranch • by Delores Fossen
When threatened by an unknown assailant, single dad Deputy Owen Slater must protect his daughter with the help of PI Laney Martin, who is investigating her sister's murder. Can they find out who is after them before someone else is killed?

#1900 TACTICAL FORCE
Declan's Defenders • by Elle James
Former marine and Declan's Defenders member Jack Snow and White House staffer Anne Bellamy must work together to stop an assassin from killing the president of the United States. But when their search makes Anne the killer's target, can they track down the criminal before he finds them?

#1901 CODE CONSPIRACY
Red, White and Built: Delta Force Deliverance
by Carol Ericson
When Gray Prescott's Delta Force commander goes AWOL under suspicious circumstances, he turns to his ex, computer hacker extraordinaire Jerrica West, for answers. But what they find might be deadly...

#1902 DEADLY COVER-UP
Fortress Defense • by Julie Anne Lindsey
With the help of bodyguard Wyatt Stone, newly single mother Violet Ames races to discover the truth about her grandmother's near-fatal accident. Before long, she'll learn that incident is part of a conspiracy long protected by a powerful local family.

#1903 BRACE FOR IMPACT
by Janice Kay Johnson
A key witness in a high-profile murder case, Maddy Kane's only chance at survival lies in the hands of former army medic Will Gannon. With armed goons hot on their trail, can they survive long enough for Maddy to testify?

#1904 IN HIS SIGHTS
Stealth • by Danica Winters
Jarrod Martin's investigation into a crime syndicate takes an unexpected turn when he joins forces with criminal heiress Mindy Kohl to protect her five-year-old niece from ruthless killers.

YOU CAN FIND MORE INFORMATION ON UPCOMING HARLEQUIN® TITLES, FREE EXCERPTS AND MORE AT WWW.HARLEQUIN.COM.

HICNM1219

"Who's in the house?" he asked.

Another head shake from Laney. "A man. I didn't see
his face."

Not that he needed it, but Owen had more confirmation
of the danger. He saw that Laney had a gun, a small
snub-nosed .38. It didn't belong to him, nor was it one
that he'd ever seen in the guesthouse where Laney was
staying. Later, he'd ask her about it, about why she hadn't
mentioned that she had a weapon, but for now they
obviously had a much bigger problem.

Owen texted his brother again, to warn him about the
intruder so that Kellan didn't walk into a situation that
could turn deadly. He also asked Kellan to call in more
backup. If the person upstairs started shooting, Owen
wanted all the help he could get.

"What happened?" Owen whispered to Laney.

She opened her mouth, paused and then closed it as
if she'd changed her mind about what to say. "About

ten minutes ago, I was in the kitchen with Addie when the power went off. A few seconds later, a man came in through the front door and I hid in the pantry with her until he went upstairs."

Smart thinking on Laney's part to hide instead of panicking or confronting the guy. But it gave Owen an uneasy feeling that Laney could think that fast under such pressure. And then there was the gun again. Where had she got it? The guesthouse was on the other side of the backyard, much farther away than the barn. If she'd gone to the guesthouse to get the gun, why hadn't she just stayed there with Addie? It would have been safer than running across the yard with the baby.

"Did you get a good look at the man?" Owen prompted.

Laney again shook her head. "But I heard him. When he stepped into the house, I knew it wasn't you, so I guessed it must be trouble."

Again, quick thinking on her part. He wasn't sure why, though, that gave him a very uneasy feeling.

"I didn't hear or see a vehicle," Laney added.

Owen hadn't seen one, either, which meant the guy must have come on foot. Not impossible, but Owen's ranch was a good half mile from the main road. If this was a thief, he wasn't going to get away with much. Plus, it would be damn brazen of some idiot to break into a cop's home just to commit a robbery.

So what was really going on?

Don't miss
A Threat to His Family *by Delores Fossen,*
available January 2020 wherever
Harlequin® Intrigue books and ebooks are sold.

www.Harlequin.com

HIEXP1219

Get 4 FREE REWARDS!

We'll send you 2 FREE Books plus 2 FREE Mystery Gifts.

Harlequin Intrigue® books feature heroes and heroines that confront and survive danger while finding themselves irresistibly drawn to one another.

FREE
Value Over
$20